# CAPTOR IN THE ATTIC

## BEAUTIFUL DECEIT SERIES
### BOOK ONE

## FELICITY BRANDON

# FREE SEXY READS

**Sign up for my newsletter and receive FREE sexy reads**
here!
https://felicitybrandonwrites.com/newsletter/

# PROLOGUE: KADE WALKER

My first kill was Laurel Turner. Blonde, with curls that never lost their bounce, she taunted me throughout my pre-pubescent years. Provoking with smiles she never intended to follow through on, Laurel goaded with furtive waves, her giggles sending fire to my blood. Those gestures portrayed a misplaced innocence. An innocence, if it truly lurked inside her, that was mine to extinguish.

I took her because I had to, because the incessant call to claim her wouldn't quiet until I did. I took her because I could—and expected it to be the end—for both of us. Someone was bound to have seen me, to have noticed me in the shadows and been suspicious. Surely, a man as young in years as I was should have left clues—a hair at the scene or a witness from an overheard conversation. Surely, I couldn't outwit the police and *get away with it*—but somehow, I did.

The authorities never caught me. No one came calling to ask for an interview or DNA. I got away with murder and in the process, got a taste for its power.

The blood lust compelled me to travel for years after that,

moving from place to place. I didn't always take a new victim, didn't always find the right woman or cede to the clamor, but when I did, I indulged myself. If anyone had bothered to look, they'd have seen a pattern emerge. Where Kade Walker went, the body count stacked up, the victims always the same—young women with pretty faces and tight bodies.

Soon, killing wasn't enough. Soon, I wanted more than only that briefest instance of influence and control. I had to own the unsuspecting woman before I took her, sought to savor all those little emotions I had no right to revel in. Murder was always too fast, but kidnapping was something else. Abduction allowed me the advantage and permitted me to play with the power I'd grasped before we reached the end, but it also changed the rules.

I was no longer gratified by only the superficial, requiring my choices to not only be attractive but also interesting. I started targeting young professionals, women with more going for them than long legs and pretty little pouts, and for a while, it was fun. I cared for them, fed them, and entertained them in the long hours of their captivity. I gave them each a piece of who I was, but ultimately, the end always came. I'd tire of her endless pleas and whimpers, and the gestures I'd once found so alluring would grate. Eventually, it was time to put her out of her misery.

This new game was riskier. Keeping the woman alive while I enjoyed her exposed me to more hazards than before, and while I thrived on danger, I grew weary of the constant challenges. I needed a new way to keep the thrills coming, something more tangible.

When I found Tiffany, everything changed.

She moved into an old house on Pennsylvania Avenue—a

huge five-bedroom place designed for a family—but now it only housed Tiffany and her cat.

I'd watched her for a while before I took the leap. After weeks of reconnaissance and getting to know her moods and routines, I liked everything I saw. Tiffany ticked all my boxes. She was intelligent and beautiful, but one thing quickly became glaringly obvious—she was always alone. I never saw her with a boyfriend and rarely witnessed her with female friends. The woman was a hermit, living only to work, then returning to feed her feline.

Her solitary lifestyle made her all the more perfect and hardened my resolve to see the plan through. Once I committed, I was there for the long haul, but the tantalizing brunette gave me all the signs this was right. She was worth the investment in energy, and soon, when the moment was right, she'd become the one thing I truly desired, the thing I'd never been able to achieve—a woman I could keep.

# CHAPTER 1: TIFFANY NOBLE

Slamming the door, I kicked off my heels and crossed the hall into the lounge. Wearily, I greeted Tabby as she slinked past my calves. She would be looking for food, but I was going to disappoint her. I couldn't wait to collapse onto my new couch, binge-watch Netflix, and spend the rest of the evening with a large glass of wine and a good book. Tabby would get fed when I did.

Every day of late was more exhausting than the last. Work had exploded into a myriad of contentious cases, all requiring my unrelenting attention to detail, and I was spending more and more hours in the office. Stretching across the soft cushions of my latest purchase, I decided enough was enough. I would have to speak to Rex about my caseload. Shadowing him was one thing, but recently, it seemed as if I was doing all the leg work while he took the lead in court. After working so damn hard on the files, it was about time I got my shot in front of the judge. I hadn't studied law all those years for this hamster wheel existence.

Sighing, I rubbed my aching feet as I contemplated what to eat. The problem with getting home so late was I could never be bothered to cook. The kitchen was one of the high-lights of the house—its enormous marble island and sparkling new fittings an undoubted draw when I'd snapped up the place—but these days, I was barely there and rarely benefited from the fancy refurb.

Reaching for the remote, I decided it would have to be takeout again. I was too tired to cook and even less inter-ested in cleaning up afterward. Pulling out my mobile, I clicked on the app, which promised to deliver food within thirty minutes, selecting the first few items and completing the order. One of these days, I would get myself together. I'd come home at a decent time and prepare a proper meal. Hell, maybe one day there would be *someone* to come home to.

Shaking my head, I flicked through the channels on the huge flat-screen television. The surround sound echoed around me, enveloping me in the array of entertainment. Incredibly demanding my profession may be, but it afforded me all the comforts I could desire. I lived in the swankiest part of the city, drove a great car, and could buy the best of whatever I wanted. I had reasons to be grateful.

I loved the house, had yearned for it from the first moment I saw the details, but couldn't deny it had its quirks. It was only thirty or so years old, but it made the most pecu-liar noises, especially from the attic. When I'd first moved in, I'd put it down to the plumbing, but more than one workman had told me everything was fine in that department. I'd contacted pest control, believing there had to be an infesta-tion of birds or something else that had taken a shine to the eaves, but again, no professional had found evidence of drop-pings or scratching. It seemed the place had a will of its own and the beating heart resided in the loft.

Deciding never to venture up there again, when I was home alone—which was most of the time—I insisted on having background noise. Television or radio usually suffced to dull out the strange sounds, the white noise becoming my new normal.

Sinking onto the sofa, I sensed myself dozing, the weight of the day finally lifting now I was home. My breathing slowed as my phone slipped from my fingers, and even though I could still hear the television blaring in the background, the noise was not enough to disturb my nap.

The dream came again, easing my world into monochrome as I tried to fathom its reasoning. It was always the same. I was there in the house, but I wasn't safe. I never saw the cause of my paranoia, but the sense of unease was unmistakable, escalating in my stomach until it filled my chest.

Fleeing my bedroom, I ran down the hall in only my nightshirt, conscious of my rapidly pounding heart. Something was after me. I could feel the weight of its stare, but glancing nervously over my shoulder, there was nothing.

There was always nothing.

Sprinting down the galleried staircase, I headed for the door. Every fiber of my body screamed I was in danger—to get out of this house—but as I approached the entrance, my body became heavy and uncoordinated, as if each limb was made of lead. Struggling to lift my feet, I dragged them slowly toward the front door. I could see my escape, could reach for the handle, but could never get there. My motion was protracted as though the floor had morphed into gum, and it was impossible to take another step.

"No!" I screamed, releasing some of the tension in the pit of my belly. "Not again!"

The nightmare burgeoned, presenting me with the

inevitable quandary. I was in trouble from an invisible threat, yet I couldn't move. I was never allowed to leave. The object of my desire was right there for the taking, but the house would not permit me to take it. The door may as well be a hundred miles away for all the hope I had of reaching it. Frustration furled inside until I couldn't take another breath.

That's when I heard it—heard him. The unmistakable sound of a man's voice breathing down my neck and raising all the tiny hairs there.

"Tiffany."

Opening my lips, I wanted to scream, but my fear snatched the sound, and my ears strained to hear the next haunting call.

"Tiff-any."

God, I didn't want to look around, didn't want to see whoever was there, but I had no choice. Immobilized to the spot, I glanced down at my body to find I was naked, the shirt I'd worn ripped away, although I hadn't noticed the deed.

"Tiff-any."

I shivered at his growl, knowing what must be done yet still too terrified to glance behind me. Nothing good could come from facing the owner of that voice, nothing that took me closer to freedom, but even as I wrestled with the dilemma, my head turned. It moved as though it had a will of its own as if the stranger with the commanding tone compelled it. My heart threatened to leap into my throat as my gaze gradually crawled to where his voice had come from. Who was this man? Why was he in my house?

"Tiffany!"

I jerked from my spot, able to move only an inch as I realized he'd moved, his voice now coming from some other indiscernible location in the room.

"What?" I screeched, finally able to force the words from my lips. "What do you want from me?"

"Tiffany."

The sound morphed, and my brows furrowed as I tried to understand the difference. It took a moment for me to appreciate it was no longer my name I heard but something else—another noise—a hard and insistent tapping that demanded to be answered.

Heart hammering, I woke up. My eyes flew open in panic, my gaze frantically searching the room for any sign of a threat, but there was nothing. The television was still deafening, and the evening light had bled into darkness while I'd slept, but everything else was the same. I was safe.

Sliding my feet from the couch, the sound of knocking captured my attention again, and this time, I realized what it was—someone was knocking at the front door. Finding my phone on the rug, it wasn't difficult to conclude who.

"Coming!" I yelled as I raced toward the door, the feat easy now I was no longer hampered by the constraints of my repeating nightmare.

"Hi!" I smiled as I yanked the door open to find the impatient delivery driver. It wasn't Jed, my normal guy. The stranger's angry glower conveyed how long he must have been waiting. "I'm sorry."

"No problem," he replied through gritted teeth as he thrust the paper bag into my chest. "Enjoy your meal."

"Thanks."

I shut the door behind me, grateful he wasn't there to witness my embarrassment. What the hell was wrong with me? When I wasn't working, I seemed to be stuck in the same incessant dream. I knew the scenes so well, they replayed in my head even when I wasn't sleeping.

"I must be going mad," I muttered, carrying my food to

the huge mahogany dining table. Pulling back a chair, I sank into it, pulling out a cold fry and munching on one end as Tabby appeared in the doorway. I didn't know why I'd bought such grandiose dining furniture since I was the only one who ate there, but something about the paradox struck a chord in my head. The house and furniture were reminiscent of my entire life—expensive and empty.

Blowing out a long breath, I ripped open the bag and unwrapped the burger. Perhaps I'd skip the binge-watch after all and just feed Tabby, then run myself a hot bath. More than ever, I needed a decent night's sleep.

# CHAPTER 2: KADE

Always present, I was the watcher. I held her hand in the darkness. I dried her tears. I was her everything, and even if, at this stage, those things were only figments of my imagination, they were prophetic inventions. I knew what was coming around the corner and was happy to wait. I was the omnipresent shadow, the gaze from the corner of the room—her dark protector—the guardian angel she didn't even know she had. My lips curled at the thought.

Naturally, she never saw me, never noticed where I hid. It is true what they say—people only see what they want to see, what they *expect* to see, and Tiffany was no exception. Beautiful, intelligent, and alluring, Tiffany was quite the spectacle, but she was not an explorer. She chose not to investigate the sounds in the attic, aside from the few irritating tradesmen who'd trailed around before leaving with their tails between their legs. I sent them away with nothing, leaving her to persuade herself that it was only the wind she'd heard or the noises of an expanding house.

She saw the flickering television screen, the resonance of

the damn thing growing louder with each day, and she felt the soft purring cat as it wrapped its way around her ankles, but she was not aware of me. Or perhaps she only chose not to be. Like the demon lurking in the dark, maybe the threat of who I was, was simply too much, but that was how I liked it. I would watch. I would wait until it was time to make my move.

The hours of daylight were all mine, time when I could move freely around the property and relax. I liked to sleep in her bed, breathing in her intoxicating scent as I slipped between her cotton sheets. If the excitement of being there became too much, I would take care of the need, ensuring her bedding had time to dry before she returned home. Regardless, I would leave the bed exactly as she had left it, taking photographs to ensure consistency.

The daytime also afforded me preparation, an opportunity to check and replace the multiple mini cameras I had set up around Tiffany's home and enjoy the footage I'd collected. Many a happy hour was spent in her bed, rewatching those tiny gestures that drove me wild—the way she tucked her hair behind her ears when she concentrated or how fabulous she looked when she undressed—those were the things I valued as I hit pause and rewind. One day I would witness those gestures firsthand, would have her come and crawl at my command—but I was jumping ahead of myself. We were still a long way from that, and I intended to enjoy every day between now and then.

I smiled as that idea reverberated, and ensuring her bedroom was just how I had found it, I sped down the stairs to the kitchen. Tiffany's house was wonderful, and I gave her full credit for both the purchase and the way she'd dressed it. It was just as well. For my plan to work, I couldn't leave its confines, couldn't risk being seen sneaking in or out by a do-good neighbor, which meant the house had become my prison. Of course, I reveled in its luxuries, in the gigantic spa bath and the refrigerator crammed with food. I didn't know why she bought the preposterous number of groceries she did, but I was grateful, careful to never take enough to concern her.

Not that I needed to worry. Tiffany seemed increasingly frazzled, the job that drew her from my clutches most days dominating her time. Distracted and apparently unable to commit to anything except work and her bed, she barely noticed when I loomed in the corner and barely flinched when I stroked her soft skin. These days, I was growing so bold, I'd even taken to calling her name, just a gentle murmur while she slept. My cock hardened at the realization of how close my dream had come to fruition. After scheming for so long, she was within grasping distance.

Unlike the object of my affection, my intentions were not founded on diversion or denial but on solid planning and attention to every detail. When I struck, not only did the timing have to be right, but every aspect had to be perfect. There could be nothing but the best for Tiffany and for the life we would build together. The finale of this act would be flawless.

Siphoning a few grapes, slices of bread, and peanut butter, I enjoyed a late lunch as I surveyed the room. The house was clean, I would give Tiffany that, but it lacked a homely feel—the product of a woman who spent too much time in the office. Rolling my eyes, I finished my sandwich and lowered to my haunches to greet the cat. Once upon a time, the animal had riled me, but I had come to see her as an ally. She, like me, was ignored by a disinterested Tiffany, but unlike her feline companion, I would not be placated with the occasional caress.

I would demand everything from her.

Glancing around the kitchen, I cleaned and tidied where I had been, deciding everything had been put back in the correct place. She'd never cottoned on to the fact I was living there, but I didn't want today to be the day she was enlightened. Better my exquisite angel remained wonderfully naïve to her fate—until I decided otherwise.

Wandering from the kitchen, I took in the vast open hallway. The dark wood paneling might have been oppressive in a smaller space, but the open gallery style spoke of elegance and wealth. I had grown to admire the interior design over the time I'd lived with her, approving its sophisticated charm, but there was one aspect that continually vexed me.

*Flowers.* What this place needed was fresh flowers—something wonderful to illuminate the space. Why would a woman with her obvious money and taste never buy them for herself? Perhaps she had been raised to believe it was churlish to indulge in such things, but if that was the case, I would have to vehemently disagree. An attractive bloom could bring a room to life, as well as add a sweet, floral fragrance. It was exactly what the place required. I concluded then and there, I would buy them for her. A girl like Tiffany needed class and splendor. Pulling out my phone, I went online to select the ideal bouquets, and it didn't take long for me to select the right blooms.

Satisfied with my work, I ushered the cat away as I strode to the window. Being holed up in the attic was the price I had to pay for the life I wanted, but there were downsides. Staring at the sun, I was reminded of the biggest one. I never got to feel its warmth and comfort anymore, couldn't be consoled by its nourishing rays. Tiffany was worth it—I had no doubt about that—but there were times I longed to burst onto the decking and ignore the consequences.

"One day," I whispered, watching as my breath steamed the glass. "One day, I shall take what's mine and be free."

Turning at the reassuring thought, I wandered to the foot of the stairs. Tiffany was rarely home early, but I couldn't run the risk of being discovered should she suddenly decide to surprise me. I could occupy myself on the second floor for a while, rifling through her possessions and relishing her substantial selection of sex toys until it was time to ascend to my evening resting place. There I would watch her monotonous routines play out before she finally collapsed in bed.

Tiffany attracted me more than any other woman I'd known, but if there was one thing I would alter, it was her dull predictability. Her routine never changed and tonight was no different from any other. Stumbling in just after seven, she crumpled on the sofa for the fourth night running before ordering more take out. It was a mystery to me why a person with so much fresh food should need to consume so much high-fat, processed nonsense. It was behavior I would change once she belonged to me, but in the short term, I was forced to witness the ordeal, watching her pollute her wonderful body as she shoveled fried chicken between her lips.

One aspect was different though—the absence of the incessant television. Instead, I watched from the various secret cameras littered around her house as she took a new bottle of wine upstairs with her laptop and settled on her bed. Adrenaline coursed through my system as I recalled how I had pleasured myself in the same spot only a matter of hours before. The reality was all the sweeter when she logged on to one of her favorite fetish sites and found her own release. My cock swelled at the sublime sight of her writhing and mewling on the bed as if she was there only for my viewing pleasure, knowing someday she would do more than tease.

Her need satiated, she paused the video playing on her laptop and went to run herself a bath. I took the chance to zoom in on the screen, grinning at what I found. As if I required further proof that she was made for me, Tiffany had been pleasuring herself to the sight of heavy-duty bondage. The woman paused on-screen was spread-eagled over a table while plugged and exposed. A huge gag had been shoved between her lips while her antagonist tormented her pleasing body.

Stroking my erection, I imagined Tiffany in the anonymous blonde's place, envisioning her wide blue eyes as she realized she was helplessly fettered and powerless to prevent whatever happened next. Between us, we had the perfect tools for the job. Tiffany had quite the toy box stashed by her bed, including a gratifying array of gags, plugs, and dildos, and I hadn't wasted my time while I'd been hidden in her attic.

I'd ordered the very best bondage, paying for specific timed deliveries to ensure only I was here when they were pushed through her letterbox. When I finally decided to push the button and seize her, Tiffany wouldn't know what hit her. I was the living embodiment of everything she fantasized about, while she was my ideal partner.

"Jeez," I murmured, amazed at how rapidly the mental image had aroused me. I wouldn't be able to hold back much longer the way things were going, which was why it was so perfect when the doorbell rang—right on cue.

I checked my watch excitedly, glad to see my first floral tribute was on time as she pulled on her robe and ran down the stairs to answer it. No doubt, Tiffany was confused by the latest intrusion. Her daily dose of junk food had already been ordered and consumed, and I suspected she wasn't expecting anything else. But *I* was. I turned up my phone's audio as I tuned into the hallway camera.

"Hey, delivery for Tiffany."

"Er, yes, that's me." Her brows knitted as the delivery guy pushed the enormous bouquet into her hands. "But I didn't order any flowers."

"Must be from a secret admirer." He laughed with a shrug. "Maybe there's a note?"

"Yeah," she replied as she eyed the ornamental orchid. "I guess."

I just caught sight of his nonchalant expression before she closed the door and wandered to the kitchen. Switching camera views, I held my breath as she placed the orchid on the counter. It was delicate and beautiful—just like her—a living thing that needed to be tended to and nurtured. Tiffany was the essence of that flower—desperate to bloom into something greater if only someone would take the time to help her grow. Fortunately for her, I was that someone.

She searched for a note, but of course, there wasn't one. When I had something to say to Tiffany, I would do so in person and would make sure she had no choice but to hear me.

# CHAPTER 3: TIFFANY

"Well, this is weird," I mumbled, finally giving up my search and standing back to admire the orchid. It was beautiful, its delicate and ornate white petals coveted by many, but why the hell had it been delivered to me? Orchids weren't my choice. There was no note with the flower, and the guy who'd brought it had been clueless. "Maybe it was delivered to the wrong address."

Yes, that must be it. It's a mistake, but a pretty one.

Smiling, I flicked off the light and climbed the stairs to my bedroom. Perhaps the floral service would notice the error and come calling tomorrow, and if they didn't, I'd keep the orchid. They weren't my favorite bloom, but they were beautiful.

I flushed as I wandered back into the room, my gaze drinking in my abandoned laptop and messy covers. Catching my lower lips between my teeth, I remembered how incredible the pleasure had been before the interruption, but the moment had definitely passed. I'd worked hard to shake off the shackles of my religious upbringing, convincing myself there was nothing sinful or wrong about self-love, but guilt still twisted in my belly as I surveyed the scene.

Tidying away the evidence, as if persuading myself I had nothing to be ashamed of, I plugged in my MacBook and shook the robe from my shoulders. I watched as the silk pooled at my feet. Sighing, I stepped into the tub, sliding down and stretching out in its substantial length. It had been another long day, and there would be more to come tomorrow, but after my orgasm, I hoped to finally get some rest.

I lurched bolt upright with a scream, my head pounding as I fisted the sheets. *Shit!* The same nightmare flooded my brain, the view of the unreachable door still fresh in my memory.

I'd been so close to grasping it, my fingers only an inch from the prize, though every time I strained to reach it, I seemed to get farther away while the ominous sense of menace approached from behind. The unseen oppressor, a nameless and neverending threat.

"I can't keep doing this." Resting my face in my palms, I tried to calm my racing heart, but it was useless. Rather than learning to control the dream, the fear was intensifying. Glancing down at my body, I noticed I was soaked in sweat. "I have to get a grip."

Slipping from the sheets, I padded to the en suite and flicked on the overhead light. I blinked at its glare as I walked to the bathroom cabinet, where my weary expression reflected back to me. At thirty-six, I was in good shape, or at least I had been when I'd had time to go to the gym. Staring, I tried to decide what had happened to that woman. My dark hair clung to my face, framing large, tired eyes. I vaguely looked like the Tiffany I'd once been, but not much. Increasingly, I was a different person, distracted and constantly drained. No wonder I wasn't getting to lead the big cases at work. I was exhausted, and it was showing. Maybe Rex was worried I couldn't handle the pressure. The thought knotted inside me, both paranoia and irritation burgeoning in equal measure.

"I'm too old to be having nightmares," I declared, tugging the doors of the cabinet open. Pulling in a deep breath, I reviewed the array of over-the-counter drugs. Surely, there was something to help me sleep. I used to take a mild sedative to aid rest, but scanning the line of drugs, I realized the product was missing.

"I must have finished it." I sighed, cursing myself for not being more organized, another consequence of my weariness and workload. "Chamomile tea it is."

I sighed, resigned to trudge back to the kitchen if it meant I might actually get a few more hours of sleep. I had a coffee maker in the bedroom, but a shot of caffeine was the last thing I needed.

Closing the cabinet doors, I was just turning to leave the bathroom when a dark silhouette caught my eye. A tall shadow figure loomed behind me, its presence visible in the mirrored door. *Oh God!* My pulse sped up as I looked harder, certain I must be hallucinating in my half-asleep state, but to my horror, I found it was still there, leaning against my open bedroom door.

Time protracted as I spun around, my rational mind already convincing me of all the reasons my eyes were wrong, while my imagination fought to run away from the terror. *The house must be haunted!* That would explain all the odd noises I'd heard and the unnerving sense I was often watched. Facing the door, I stumbled forward, ignoring the insistent hammering of my heart.

Where was it?

Straining to see where the shadow had gone, I flicked on the main bedroom light and searched behind the door and under the bed, but there was nothing. No one. No intruder and certainly no ghost.

But I knew what I'd seen… or at least, I *thought* I'd known.

"Crap." I shivered as I stripped out of my damp nightshirt and wrapped my robe around myself. "I really must need help if I'm seeing things that aren't there."

It was going to take more than tea to remedy whatever was wrong with me.

"I'll make an appointment with the doctor in the morning," I promised aloud, as though the house would bear witness to my vow. "This can't go on."

Collapsing onto the bed, I tugged the cover over me. Half of me was desperate for rest, while the other half was frightened to go back to sleep, but my head was so heavy, I suspected I knew which half would win. Closing my eyes, I steadied my breathing as I tried to dismiss my fears. The Chamomile would have to wait. I needed something much stronger.

Kade

I waited in the darkness, expecting her to go downstairs and make some grim-smelling herbal tea to help her sleep. That was the usual routine. Pressed against the wall, my heart beating with excitement, I delayed any advance until I was sure there was no chance she'd leave the bedroom. The minutes bled into the best part of an hour before I crept back to her side.

Tiffany was sleeping at the foot of her bed, curled up into a ball. I approached with care, not wanting to disturb but wanting to be close—always wanting to get closer.

Had she seen me from the bathroom earlier? Was it my reflection that had caused her panicked return? My lips curled as I replayed the event in my head. It had certainly seemed as if she'd spotted something. Perhaps I'd been visible from the bathroom light, but my deft ability to slink into the shadows had likely heightened her confusion. She was tired —she was always tired. She'd only *thought* she'd seen someone. It was all in her mind. The thought was more amusing than it should have been. I would possess the woman and make her mine, but it was cruel to torment her this way. Still, I couldn't help the glee that rose at the memory of her frantic wide eyes or the way she'd lurched into the bedroom. I craved that urgency from her. It was what I deserved.

"Tiffany."

I settled by her bed, breathing in her tantalizing scent. Lifting one hand, my fingertips grazed over the length of her hair. I wished I could just grab a fistful of the tresses the way I desired.

"Soon," I promised, forcing my hand to withdraw. There had been enough excitement for one night, and I couldn't risk waking her again, but the lure of the woman was unfathomable. I couldn't leave her, couldn't waste the hours we had together. One day, she would realize the extent of my devotion. She'd understand whatever depravity dominated her fantasies when she came apart at her own touch was nothing compared to what I would do to her.

*Fuck.* My jaw tightened as the dull monotony of my predicament fell over me again. I was close, so close to having everything I sought, but still, I was light-years from my need. Exasperation soared as frustration furled in my stomach. Whatever I was going to do, I had to do it soon. Resting my head against the mattress, we were only a few inches from each other, but it might as well have been oceans. I couldn't stand many more nights like this. The time for action approached.

This was the calm before the carnage.

# CHAPTER 4: TIFFANY

It was gone eight o'clock by the time I wrestled my bags to the front door, far later than I wanted to be home, but I'd opted to stay late to compensate for my tardiness this morning. My impromptu nighttime scare had sent me into a deep sleep, and I hadn't heard my alarm go off. As a result, I'd been almost an hour late for work, which hadn't gone unnoticed by Rex.

Night was already closing in around me as I slipped my key into the door and slung my case into the hall. My late arrival also meant I hadn't gotten around to calling the doctor, and now, faced with another dark and lonely night, I regretted my inaction. Whatever was wrong with me, I needed to get some rest. Insomnia, as it turned out, didn't suit me.

Heaving in a breath, I turned to collect my briefcase and saw it—an orchid sat on my porch. Brows knitting, I crouched to grab the flower.

"What's this?"

I glanced around as if one of my neighbors had left it

there and was waiting to jump out and surprise me. *That wasn't bloody likely.* I'd lived here for just under a year and was yet to properly meet most of the people who lived on my street. *That's what you get from working endless hours.*

"Another orchid?"

This was getting strange. I didn't mind the fragile flower, but I wouldn't order one and certainly hadn't asked for two. Grabbing the tiny pot, I lifted the flower and reached for my briefcase, striding inside and shutting the door with my foot.

"There must be a card this time," I demanded, though I wondered who I was trying to convince.

Dropping my case, I carried the orchid into the kitchen and placed it next to the first one. I'd been in such a fluster this morning, I hadn't even thought about taking it from its packaging, but since no one seemed to have asked for it back and I now had another, there seemed no harm in opening the flowers. Reaching for my kitchen scissors, I cut the transparent wrapping away from both orchids, throwing the plastic away while I considered them. They were different orchids, the former producing smaller, white flowers, while the most recent delivery blossomed with larger pink petals.

I shook my head as I wandered toward my ever-depleting wine rack. Choosing a bottle of red, I twisted the cap open. At the rate I was drinking, I'd have to restock soon, but the thought did little to appease me. It had been one hell of a day, and the unexpected gift was the final straw. I needed a drink. Finding a clean glass, I poured the wine, enjoying the look of its rich burgundy body before I took a sip.

Strolling to the sofa, I sank into its comfortable confines as I mulled over the many conundrums. Tomorrow was Friday, which meant there was still time to speak to the doctor before the weekend. If I turned in early and got a good night's sleep, I could leave the office on time. If I was truly lucky, I could even meet Melissa for a meal after work. I relaxed at the idea, pulling my phone from my pocket and typing a quick text to my friend. It would be lovely to see her, and I was sure I'd feel more like myself once I was out of the house. I could tell her about my peculiar orchid deliveries and see what she made of them. Melissa had always been a practical woman. She was bound to have some good advice.

Smiling, I gulped my wine, allowing its soothing bouquet to console me. I vaguely recalled draining the glass before the desire to sleep became overwhelming.

"Tiffany." His voice was soft, but I recognized the timbre at once. It was the same tone I had heard countless times before, the same man who called to me as I slept, but that couldn't be right, could it? That man was a menace, a low murmur that filled me with escalating dread. This couldn't be the same man.

"What?" I awoke, though a part of me must have realized I was still dreaming. "Who are you?"

"I'm here." He sounded pleased, as though I should be grateful. "To guard you."

"Who are you?" He wasn't listening, and aside from the terror his presence evoked, my frustration simmered. Why wasn't he listening?

"You know me."

I sensed the smile in his voice.

"If you don't, you will."

"What's that supposed to mean?" I sat up, glancing around, though I couldn't decide where I was. Darkness permeated from every corner, disguising my location as well as it hid his intent.

"It means you need to stop running." His voice was louder as if he'd moved closer, but I hadn't heard him move. Had I? I didn't recall any movement, but then my head was fuzzy, an exhausting mix of sleep deprivation and wine. "You just need to give in."

This time, his words came from just ahead, and I envisioned a man looming there in front of me, shielded by the darkness.

"Give in to what?" Christ, I was so tired, I was having actual conversations with a figment of my imagination. Things were getting worse.

"To me."

I gasped at his sudden proximity, sensing whoever he was, he was standing right in front of me. "I-I don't understand," I panted, easing away from him.

I'd fallen asleep on the couch, but it appeared I was on a hard floor, the cracks between the boards obvious as I dragged myself backward. Something else was strange as well, the odd metallic dragging sound that echoed as I shifted.

"You will," he promised, and the surety in his velvety tone twisted the knot of anxiety tighter in my belly.

Something wasn't right. Something was terribly wrong.

"What's happening?"

It sounded ridiculous saying it out loud, but I couldn't fathom who he was, where we were, or what was going on. Not that it mattered since it was just another dream—another nightmare—like all those I'd endured over the last few weeks. I'd find myself at the front door soon enough and wake myself up screaming. I just had to ride out the intensity of this new scenario. I just had to—

"Quiet now." There was an insidious edge to his voice I

hadn't noticed before, a sign of someone nefarious. "I want silence."

I tensed, wanting to rebuke his gruff tone but sensing it was better to comply.

"Finally, I have you, Tiffany." There was no denying the glee radiating from his voice.

"Wh-What do you mean?"

"I said, quiet." He rushed at me, dropping to his knees, and even though I couldn't see his face, I sensed how close he was.

Panic spiked, urging me back, and unthinkingly, I dragged myself backward, aware of the peculiar trailing noise that followed... then the realization dawned. *I* made that sound, or something attached to me was making it every time I moved.

"You won't get far in that direction."

I shivered at his dark chuckle.

"I chose this spot for a good reason."

Inching away from whatever danger he represented, my fingertips skimmed the edge of something hard behind me. My heart raced as they grazed the curved surface, and in my mind's eye, I imagined the baseboard between the interior wall and the floor. The thought was reinforced as my hand rose, brushing over something unyielding. What was it? I glanced back in my terror, my brow furrowing. What hindered my escape? My dreams had never been like this before.

"See what I mean?" There was a horrible smug sound to his tone. "You have nowhere to go."

My palm traced up the hard surface, the answer to my riddle finally confirmed—a wall! I was trapped by a wall.

"Oh God." My throat dried as the awful reality washed over me like freezing water. Wherever I was, I had just backed myself against a wall. Rising on unsteady legs, I frantically fought for composure.

"Silly girl," he sneered, then he was on me. Hard, powerful thighs pressed into me, one hand edging my shirt higher on my hip. "What did I tell you?"

Alarm erupted at his touch, an acknowledgment that whoever this was, he was real enough, as was his intent.

"I-I..." I started, though I had no idea what I was going to say. The horror bursting in my mind was making it impossible to think.

"I told you to be quiet," he articulated as his chest moved closer to pin me against the wall. "Remember?"

The creeping hand at my thigh halted only an inch from my sex. My frightened mewl was the only acknowledgment of its journey.

"I asked you a question." His voice lowered to a low snarl, producing a fresh gasp from me. "Now, you can answer."

"Y-Yes," I stammered, haunted by how big and strong he was. I couldn't discern his features in the shadows, but he felt enormous and undeniably powerful. The thought was beyond disconcerting. "I remember."

"And?" He sounded unimpressed. "What did I ask?"

"For me to be quiet."

I wished I could put up more of a fight like the women I'd seen in those Hollywood action movies. I'd liked to have headbutted the bastard and kung-fu kicked him across the floor. This was a dream.... wasn't I supposed to be able to do those things in my unconscious? The sad reality was I didn't put up any fight, could barely even pull in each breath. His presence was captivating and utterly terrifying.

"So, you do recall?" He laughed, a dark noise that seemed to echo from every direction, and all at once, his face closed in on mine, the heat of his minty breath conveying his growing proximity. "That's good."

Christ, he must have only been a few inches from me, his hips pinning me in place as his other hand rose to my face. I panted as his palm pressed lightly to my cheek, one finger sliding down to cradle my chin.

"That means you *can* listen."

I sensed his smile.

"*Can* be taught."

"Who are you?" I tried again, desperate to break out of this hypnotic and disturbing dream. "Please, I don't understand."

Silence swelled in what little space passed between us, and in that heavy quiet, terror bloomed. What had I done by speaking? Hadn't he just reiterated he wanted me to be quiet? Why couldn't I just fucking listen?

"I'm sorry!" I was close to tears as the apology spilled from my lips, confusion mingling with dread.

"Tiffany."

My name vibrated down my body, and to my horror, I noticed the way my nipples beaded at his gravelly tone.

"You will learn." The hand at my chin dipped to my collar bone, and before I could pull in another decent breath, his fingers wrapped around my windpipe. "I promise you that."

"Please!"

If I'd thought I'd known panic, this moment assured me just how wrong I'd been. He held me by the neck, my life literally suspended in the palm of his hand, but his grip didn't tighten.

"Even now, that mouth cannot be quiet." He sounded amused by the idea, but it was little consolation when his grip was held steadfast around my windpipe. "I must see what I can do to help you with that." His face neared, his lips skimming first my temple, then lowering along the ridge of my nose. I could scarcely breathe as his lips grazed over mine. "I'm sure I can think of a way."

*Fuck.* The word resonated in my head as his lips moved, first caressing, then demanding a kiss. What was I supposed to do? I didn't know who the guy was, let alone assent to this behavior, but with his unforgiving body pressed into mine and his hand still at my throat, there was little choice but to succumb. With a small yelp, I acquiesced, permitting my lips to part as he took what he wanted, and God help me, it was the most passionate exchange I could remember. Heat furled in my core as his tongue snaked into my mouth. His free hand caressed my hip as he plundered my mouth.

*What's wrong with me?* The question echoed as I melted into his touch. How could I find this even slightly arousing? When I finally saw my doctor, perhaps it was time to ask for a psychological referral.

"Better," he snarled as he drew away. "I've learned something new about you, Tiffany."

I panted, not daring to speak again, although a part of me wondered if I defied him, would he kiss me again?

"Now, I know how much you like hard, ruthless kisses."

Oh God, had he really just said that?

"That's useful information." The hand at my throat stiffened a fraction, and whatever excitement had surfaced was chased away by terror. "I want to learn everything I can about you."

What the fuck did that mean?

A strangled gasp left my lips as his grip stiffened. This wasn't sexy, and it sure as hell didn't seem to be leading to anything I would enjoy. It was time to wake up. Tugging the hand trapped between our bodies, I pushed against his chest with all my might, but it was futile. The man was obviously made of muscle and didn't even flinch at my exertion.

"Wake up!" I urged myself, my breathing ragged as I fought for air. "Wake up, Tiff."

His eerie laughter rang out, ratcheting up my dread to a whole other level.

"Now, little girl, what makes you think you're sleeping?"

# CHAPTER 5: KADE

What I would have given for a little illumination at that moment. My soul ached to see her shock. Even one flickering candle would have been enough to reveal her expression, but I imagined those wide, blue stunned eyes as she flustered against the wall.

"What do you mean?"

Even with my fingers curled around her throat, she still couldn't quiet that magnificent mouth. It made me wonder which of the sexy gags she had stashed in her bedroom would be the first to be forced between her lips. Fuck, I couldn't wait to hear the noises she made once it was in place.

"You're not dreaming, darlin'." Perhaps it was for the best that she couldn't see my smirk. "I *am* here. This is real, and it's happening."

"Wh-What?" Her breaths were coming hard and fast. "I-I don't understand."

How many times had she intimated that already? I had to be sympathetic to the gorgeous little brunette and remember while I had been planning this wonderful finale for months while she was completely out of the loop.

"I'm serious, little girl." My thumb grazed her windpipe. She was so tiny and vulnerable, it wouldn't take much to squeeze and bring this whole adventure to an abrupt halt. Another version of Kade would have been inclined to do so, but fortunately for Tiffany, that man was no longer me. I had another intention altogether. "If you can't keep that pretty little mouth shut, I will."

Seizing her in the darkness, I dragged her away from the wall and forced her away from the eaves. Luckily for her, her attic was a huge and expansive space, so there was room for her tantrum. She went just as I'd expected, panting and screaming with her heels smashing into the floor whenever she could find traction. The shackles I'd attached to her limbs crashed against the wood floor, adding volume, but I only laughed at her pitiful performance. If Tiffany thought this would save her, she was in for a massive blow. All such displays would earn her was more time in my choice of punishment.

"There."

I shoved her to the floor, carpeted in this part of the attic. I'd left her in the shadows of the eaves while she'd slept off the cocktail of sedative-laced wine she'd drank earlier. The sleeping tablets I'd borrowed from the master en suite cabinet had certainly proved to be useful, but now it was time for illumination. Moving to the wall, I flicked on the sidelight.

Her gaze darted around frantically, her hand rubbing her throat and her brows knitting when she saw the metal on her wrists. "Wh-What are these?"

"You know what they are." My tone was dry. "You spend

enough time thinking about them." I enjoyed her face blanching now that the attic was lit.

"C-Cuffs." She could hardly get the words out.

"That's right." A jolt of electricity raced along my spine. I'd waited for this moment for so long. The realization in her gaze was scintillating.

"Why am I wearing cuffs?" Her attention shifted from the metal bracelets to my face.

"I want you in them." I lifted my chin. *Because you want them, too.* My lips twitched as the final line repeated in my head.

"B-But…" Her chest rose and fell even faster. "You can't do this! You can't—"

"Let me stop you right there." Triumph soared as she ceded. The shock shining in her eyes was almost as exquisite as her horrified expression. "I *can* do whatever I choose." I slowed my pace, enjoying the experience I'd waited so long for. "Things will go much more smoothly for you if you learn to accept that early on." I watched as some of the pieces fell into place.

"The attic?"

Honestly, I should have been incensed about her inability to shut up—especially after the warnings I had given her—but frankly, I was having too much fun. This was the culmination of months of plotting and biding my time. I wanted to savor every fucking second.

"Your attic," I clarified with a smile. "Where I've been living."

Her lips parted as if she was going to push her luck and speak further, but there were no words.

"That's right," I confirmed, reading her shell-shocked visage. "It's been me all along. Those noises you've been hearing, the ones you've denied and tried to ignore… that was me."

"What do you want?" As if I'd just thrown cold water over her, she shuffled backward, her eyes as wide as saucers.

"Wrong question," I assured her. "And that's certainly not how you address me, little girl."

Maybe I'd been hasty calling for silence when it was this entertaining seeing her scramble for clues. There would be a time for all those delicious gags, but not now.

"I don't even know who you are."

She rose on her elbows, eyeing me wildly as she attempted to climb to her knees, but only one long stride from me was enough to topple her back to the carpet. The poor little thing was presumably still woozy from the drugs. She'd need rehydrating—once I'd had my enjoyment.

"I am your Master." I don't know how I suppressed my grin as I announced my title. It was as arrogant as it was inaccurate. The Watcher would have been far more appropriate.

"*Master?*" she spat as though it left a bad taste in her mouth. "Are you serious?"

"Deadly serious." I lowered to my haunches, meeting her stare head-on. "And if you want to stay alive, I suggest you use it."

"You're going to hurt me?" she asked as if she already knew the answer. "You're here to kill me."

"Nonsense." Death was the last thing on my mind. "I've come to give your life the one thing it so badly needs, Tiffany."

She pulled in a shaky breath, the gesture drawing my focus back to her fabulous chest and the stiff peaks grazing beneath the fabric of her tantalizing shirt.

"What does it need?"

"If you want answers, you'll need to use my title." I smiled, no longer caring if she saw how happy I was. "In fact, if you want anything, you'll need to use it." I paused, watching her responses carefully. "You get three strikes, Tiffany, then you're out."

Her eyes fluttered closed, and I got the sense she wanted to know what happened then but was too afraid—or belligerent—to ask.

"I feel sick." She clutched her belly, the color draining from her face.

"It's only the sedatives," I explained dismissively. Or the shock, though I didn't bother to vocalize the final thought.

"Sedatives?"

I arched an eyebrow, interested to see how she would respond. In the past, I had found women were compliant in the face of the gesture, but Tiffany hadn't had the chance to see me properly. She didn't yet know the beast who would tame her.

"M-Master." It looked as though it was physically painful for her to say the word, but she *had* said it, even if only under duress.

"Better." I rose to my full height, noticing the way her gaze flitted to the doorway. "I wouldn't if I were you, little girl. Any action as stupid as trying to flee will lead you straight into trouble."

"But it's my house." She closed her eyes, and I wondered if she needed to block out the sight of me before she could say the word. "Master."

"Not anymore." Of course, legally, she was right. I couldn't assume legal control of her property, but to all intents and purposes, 3645 Pennsylvania Avenue, along with everything and everyone in it, belonged to me.

"Please." She swallowed, finally climbing to her knees. I

allowed it because she looked so fucking good that way, and it was a position I was keen to keep her in. "Will you tell me your name?"

So, she wanted to know who I was? It was proof of what I already knew—Tiffany was an intelligent woman. She knew developing a rapport with her captor would lubricate the wheels, but unfortunately, she had no idea of the devil she was dealing with.

"Kade." My name echoed around the attic space. "My name is Kade, but I never want to hear you use it."

# CHAPTER 6: TIFFANY

Towering over me like a dark god, his silver-gray eyes burned with resolve.

"Kade?"

His gaze darkened. "*What* did I just say?"

"I'm sorry." I threw my palms up in an act of conciliation, aware that riling the beast would not help my course. Whoever the man was, he was an intruder—had admitted to *being* in my house.

*Of course, he's in the house.* My breathing was labored as my unhelpful monologue mocked me. *You heard him, didn't you? You even saw him! You knew something was wrong, but you did nothing.* I loathed to admit it, but I had known something was up. Between work and exhaustion, I'd allowed the thought to slide, just like so many other things.

"I'm not going to say it again."

I shivered at his low, predatory snarl.

"How do you refer to me?"

"Master."

I wanted to balk at the ludicrous term, to tell the insane moron no man was my master, but I could only force the word out, ignoring the way it stuck in my throat. I had to do what I had to do to survive. I could pay a counselor thousands of pounds to unpick the trauma at a later date.

Staring at him warily, I was suddenly conscious of how thin and short my nightshirt was. Pressing my thighs together to prevent his view, I battled the panic threatening to explode in my brain like unsupervised fireworks. This was serious—really fucking serious. There was an intruder in my house who'd already drugged and cuffed me. If that didn't give me a flavor of his intent, I didn't know what would. I was in real trouble.

I had to get out of this… out of here! Once again, my focus flitted to the attic door. If only I could get down the stairs to the phone, or better, the door, I'd be okay. A shudder rose up my spine as I acknowledged just how similar my so-called dream scenario was to my recurring nightmare. The scene that had woken me so many times in a cold sweat now seemed like my only hope. The irony might have been amusing if it hadn't been so horrifying.

"I've warned you about that." Against all odds, his tone deepened.

"I'm not doing anything," I insisted, craning my neck to meet his glare.

It was crazy to feel so vulnerable. I was in my own house —a place I'd chosen and grown to love. I knew the layout and had all of my creature comforts around me, yet this man had roared into my world and splintered it into a thousand shards of glass. Now, whichever way I looked, those shards were poised to make me bleed.

"You're looking for an escape." He actually smiled, the most terrifying gesture I'd ever seen. "I'll make it easy for you. There isn't one."

"Okay." I had to think and approach this laterally, but the

adrenaline pumping through my system was making it impossible. In the short term, I had to give him what he wanted. "What *can* I do, Master?"

"That's a better question." He took a small step toward me, the leather of his shoes nudging the edge of my knee. "The number one thing you *can* do is what I tell you to."

Oh God. I watched as he changed tack, his shoe shifting to apply pressure to my left knee. I could see what he was trying to do. He wanted my legs to part, presumably to give him access to what he really wanted. I tensed at the disturbing thought, both petrified of what he would do and perturbed by my reactions. Memories of his kiss flooded my thoughts, reminding me of how bloody good it had been. Even though he'd immobilized me, I wouldn't have fought away from that caress even if I could have.

"You'll do my bidding in the end, little girl."

My gaze rose to his smirk, and for the first time, I really looked. One thing was for sure—I didn't know Kade, but he had the sort of face I wasn't likely to forget. His tousled hair looked almost jet-black, as did the stubble decorating his chin. The color of his strangely compelling eyes was incomparable to any I'd ever seen, and his skin was stretched high over model-like cheekbones. No doubt about it, if I'd bumped into him on the street, I'd have wanted to ask him for a coffee. Kade was gorgeous.

"Please tell me what you want from me, Master."

My voice was monotone, suppressing the waves of rising panic. It didn't please me to have to use the ridiculous title, but I accepted it for what it was—a necessity if I wanted to get out of this, a reality for my survival.

He inhaled slowly as if my question had unlocked a secret door in the game we were playing. Meeting his eyes, there seemed little doubt, as far as he was concerned, this *was* a game, and I would have to learn the rules to survive.

"I just told you." He threw me a salacious smile, and despite the terror still darting in my mind, I couldn't ignore the way the gesture affected me. Kneeling in front of him, I wondered what lengths I would go to in order to be the recipient of that smile. "Weren't you listening, little girl?"

There was that term again—*little girl*—why did he keep calling me that, and why did I find it so damn enticing? A woman as capable and independent as me shouldn't be tempted by such a condescending label.

"I was listening." The words fell from my lips. "I swear it."

"So, what's the right answer?" He folded his huge arms across his broad chest, and fleetingly, I imagined just how strong and powerful his body was beneath his black attire. He'd already proved how easily he could physically over-power me. He tapped his shoe beside my foot. "I'll give you one minute to come up with it."

Fresh alarm burgeoned at the looming deadline.

"You want me to do as I'm told," I blurted, praying it was correct.

"Very good." He crouched before me, and the sight of him was nearly enough to disregard his patronizing tone. "I knew you could do it."

I gritted my teeth, holding back my sardonic retort. I hated when men treated women this way, assuming they knew better just because they were physically stronger. I'd spent my entire career trying to prove otherwise, but I had always been sexually attracted to powerful, commanding men. It wasn't something I shared with anyone else—it wasn't exactly a requisite for a shining career in law—but sexual submission was my biggest fantasy.

I glanced down at the cuffs at my wrists, trying to fathom the paradox, though I didn't know why. I'd spent a lifetime wrestling with it, and it never got easier. That's why I indulged my proclivities in private with my late-night internet sessions.

"All you need to be is obedient."

He reached for my thigh, trailing one fingertip along my goosing flesh. The attic space certainly wasn't cold, but I couldn't rationalize the reason my skin reacted to him any other way or cope with the knowledge he was alluring. Kade was the man who'd entered my personal space without permission, and looking at him, I had the sense he could do a lot more.

"You'd like that, wouldn't you?"

Wait, what—how could he know that?

"I-I don't know what you mean."

"Don't do that." His finger grazed my knee, tapping my skin as he shook his head.

"Wh-What?" My heart raced at the knowing look in his eyes.

"Don't lie to me, Tiffany."

Oh God.

"I-I…" I tried to answer but couldn't get the words to form.

"Do yourself a favor and be honest."

What the hell was I supposed to say? How could this complete stranger know anything about my deepest, darkest desires? I'd never told another living soul.

"Need me to help you?" He chuckled at my rising blush, and my hands rose to my face, cuffs and all, to shield his gaze from the heat. "No, don't do that." His hand shifted to mine, tugging at my wrist and easing my palm from my embarrassment. "Don't cover your blush., It's adorable."

*It's horrible.* The reply was on the tip of my tongue, but I didn't dare to vocalize it.

"I… I don't know what you want me to say, Master."

"Yes, you do." He smiled, placing my hands on my thighs. "I want you to tell me how the shackles make you feel."

Fuck.

"I don't know why you've put them on me." I opted to play it safe and avoid the question altogether, but honestly, I should have known better. Kade's gray eyes narrowed, and my heart hammered faster.

"How do they make you *feel?*" His growing impatience was obvious and didn't bode well.

"Scared."

That wasn't a lie. However enticing the concept seemed online, being forced into cuffs after being drugged by a man intent on keeping me captive in my house was completely overwhelming. However good-looking he was, Kade was still dangerous. He'd said he wouldn't hurt me, but what did that prove? Any man capable of breaking into my property and sedating me was accomplished enough to achieve much worse.

I shivered as that thought cemented. *He* had been in my house. I'd heard the strange noises for months. Had he been here that long? Had he been up here all that time, plotting and scheming? Oh Christ, what else had he been doing? Had he been observing me, watching me come and go, eat and sleep? Had he seen me pleasure myself? A ball of nausea tightened in my tummy, stealing my air supply. The sense of violation was crushing.

"What else?" His demand was gruff, but if I didn't know better, there was excitement glinting in his eyes.

"I don't know what else," I gasped, breathing more heavily as I contemplated the dreadful intrusion. Mental images of the things Kade might have witnessed flashed in my mind's eye, and my toes curled into the carpet as I struggled to fight back the rising emotion. He was so close, his hand less than an inch from my legs, his gaze unnervingly insistent. "Please."

"I know you're frightened." He exhaled as if trying to demonstrate how hard this was for him. I wanted to laugh at how pathetic that was. "But I want you to tell me the truth, little girl."

If it was possible, I tensed even more as the ominous term came from him again. Wrapping my arms around my chest, I huddled, willing this whole thing to be nothing more than another one of my nightmares. That must be it. This was all only a dream, and I was going to wake up at any moment. But I didn't wake up, and as the seconds ticked by, my confusion only grew. I couldn't understand how any facet of my brain was aroused by Kade and his peculiar name for me. I couldn't accept that at this most horrifying moment, when I'd just discovered the extent of his crimes, any part of me was allured.

"Tiffany."

I straightened at the warning in his tone.

"This is your last chance. Tell me how much you like bondage."

*How much I like bondage?*

His words winded me, proving what should already have been obvious. Kade must have used his time in the attic to investigate and discover much more about me than I'd realized. *He knew.* He knew I liked this stuff. He knew how I reveled in the idea of being bound and exposed. A cold chill rushed through me.

"I like the thought of it." I made myself respond. "But that's it." I met his expectant gaze, desperate for him to believe me. "I've never done anything like this, never met anyone and tried it."

"That was your second strike." He held my gaze as he answered. "You know how to refer to me by now."

Shit, I'd completely forgotten the nonsensical self-imposed title he'd demanded.

"What happens at three strikes, Master?" I finally found the courage to ask.

"You don't want to know." His lips curled into a sickening sneer as his hand skimmed the nearest metal cuff. "Or… maybe you do."

My eyes lowered to my knees, wishing the ground would open up and take me with it. Better still, I hoped it would drop him back into hell.

"I believe you've never played this way before." He tugged the cuff at my wrist, and I caught his smile in my peripheral vision. "But I know for a fact how much you like the idea."

The ball of nausea rose to my throat, compelling me to take a huge breath.

"Not like this…" I closed my eyes, knowing what I had to say next. "Master."

"Yes, like this." His reply was immediate. "Like this or any other damn way I tell you."

# CHAPTER 7: KADE

All the hours of deafening quiet and suffocating isolation, I'd dreamed about this. How would she look when she first set eyes on me? What breathy sounds would she make in her frantic anxiety? What color would her face be as she absorbed her fate? I'd pawed over the details in my mind, using them as an impetus for satisfaction, but nothing I'd imagined rivaled the reality. Nothing prepared me for the unadulterated joy of seeing her hunched and hopeless.

"I've been watching you, little girl."

No doubt, she had worked it out, but just in case she wasn't aware, I laid my cards on the table. Or, at least, I laid some of them out. She still didn't know the house was littered with cameras and didn't appreciate that a single app on my phone could take me to any location on and around her property. Tiffany had no idea how deep the rabbit hole went.

"Oh God." She choked the words, burying her face into her thighs.

"I know about your internet sessions."

Thanks to the software I'd downloaded on her laptop, I also knew precisely which sites she visited. It hadn't taken long to figure out her password. Tiffany's only flaw, as far as I could see, was her inability to think outside of the box, but that was okay. I would do the thinking from now on.

"I know the websites you use when you want to come."

She glanced up, her face flaming with mortification.

"There's no need to be embarrassed," I soothed. "Everybody does it." If they didn't, they definitely should. "I'm just saying, I understand your needs because I have those needs, as well."

"What needs do you have, Master?"

I liked how easily she had taken to using my title. It boded well for her fate if she could adapt and learn fast.

"I need to be in control." I slowed my pace, ensuring she heard—and understood—every word. "I need to dominate." *To destroy.* I held back those final words, not wishing to pulverize the woman with panic.

Tiffany blinked away tears. "You want to dominate me?"

My balls tightened at her wonderful question.

"I will dominate you," I assured her. "I like all the same things—the cuffs, the ropes, the gags…" I left the list hanging as I watched her reaction. "You and I can have some fun together."

"But…" Her hands gripped her legs so hard, her fingers were white. "What if I don't want those things?"

I had the sense she wanted to add *with you* to the end of her question, but wisely, she resisted. Falling to my knees, I reached for her hand, stroking it gently.

"If you don't, why watch those things?" I leaned closer, ensuring she had nowhere else to look except at my face. "Why do you pleasure yourself to them?"

"I don't know." She heaved in a breath as a solitary tear

broke free from her watery eyes and created a track down her cheek.

"Yes, you do." I patted the back of her hand. "You know all too well. You're just too ashamed to say."

In my experience, shame associated with sexual fantasies was all too common among women. It troubled me that Tiffany—the one *I* had chosen—had also fallen into this self-limiting pit. Many of the women I'd known would sooner be miserable and lonely than admit what turned them on, and I wouldn't let that be her destiny. Tiffany would be neither sad nor alone—not unless I decided so.

"I've never understood it, Master."

That was the closest thing to an admission I'd heard.

"I just like the thought of those things."

"I know you do," I purred, inching closer on my knees. "Tell me about them. Tell me which things specifically get you wet."

Her eyes widened as she processed the question.

"I don't find it easy to talk about this."

Well, that would have to change.

"You're going to try," I advised, easing one of her hands from her thigh and replacing it, enjoying the feeling of her smooth skin.

"Don't you already know all of this, Master?" Tiffany closed her eyes. "It seems like you do."

*Smart girl.*

"I want to hear you say them." Trailing my hand higher, I skirted under the cotton shirt she insisted on wearing.

"Please." Emotion broke in her voice as I reached her inner thigh.

"What?" I edged to her side, my free hand smoothing back her hair as my other hand caressed her leg. "I'm not hurting you, little girl."

"You're t-touching me."

Sensing how difficult it was for her to reply, my cock swelled in response to her frantic mewl.

"I'm touching what's mine. Get used to it."

Terrified blue eyes met mine.

"Answer my question," I prompted. "You don't want to get to your third strike."

"Ropes." The word came out in one long sigh. "I like the thought of being tied down."

"Hence the cuffs you own." I smiled. "And the ones I've put you in. We can try ropes, too. I have them." She didn't know it yet, but I was well prepared. "And?"

"I don't know what else, Master." Her desperation was making me even hornier.

"How about capture fantasies?" I goaded, knowing full well how often she replayed the two fake kidnap scenes she'd found online. "Do you like those?"

"Y-Yes, Master." She let out a low sob, but I ignored her misery, reveling in her confession.

"And gags? You like the thought of being silenced, don't you, little girl? Maybe with a nice big cock or with something else designed for the purpose."

"Yes." She swallowed. "It's true." Her face crumpled as the tears came faster.

I gave her a moment, merely watching as she dissolved in front of me. I thought about holding her, concluding it was too soon, so I skimmed my fingers closer to her enticing sex as my hand tightened in her hair.

"You have nothing to be ashamed about." I turned her face toward me with a fistful of her hair. "It's normal to fantasize."

"Not about these things." She struggled to get the words out, refusing to meet my eyes.

"Yes, about these things," I demanded. "I want you to be honest about how you feel, and I will insist that you are."

"I-I don't know how, Master."

I hadn't expected this part to be so damn exciting, but she was intoxicating with her wide, frightened eyes and hot body hidden under her shirt.

"You want me to keep you here, don't you?" No doubt she sensed the glee in my tone, but I no longer cared. "You want me to hold you down and make you do things?"

"No, I—"

I jerked her head backward, effectively cutting off her sentence.

"What was that?" My erection strained to be free as she winced.

"It's only a fantasy, Master," she gasped when I finally relented the pressure. "I didn't mean this. I didn't mean any of this."

"I can help you shed the guilt and shame you feel about your sexuality," I promised, clenching my fist. "Just you wait and see."

"Master." Her tiny hands rose to meet mine, the shackles hanging around her face as she attempted to relieve the strain on her scalp.

"There's no need to thank me." I would explode if I didn't take the edge off soon. "You deserve everything that's coming to you."

# CHAPTER 8: TIFFANY

*This wasn't happening.* Despite the stiff fingers wrenching my head in his preferred direction, and even though there were actual fucking shackles dangling from my wrists, there was no way this was real.

"I've spent a long time planning how to assist you."

My gaze darted to his, catching sight of his insidious grin.

"I think you'll like what I have in mind."

Panic washed over me in waves, swallowing the sounds around me as it morphed in my brain. I could hear his voice, see his lips moving, but it was difficult to pay attention to what he was saying. Suddenly, all I could see, hear and taste was terror.

"You don't have to worry." His lips curled into a new sinister smile as his fingers stroked my chin.

Beneath my night shirt, my nipples beaded, no doubt a product of the dread unfurling in my belly and the temperature at this time of night. I refused to accept it was anything more, denying the possibility that any part of me was excited by this sickening turn of events.

This man—this predator—had been hiding in my house

and watching me. My stomach churned at the awful violation. How had this happened? How had I not noticed and notified the authorities, and more to the point, what the hell was I going to do?

"I'm going to take care of you." He swooped, collecting me and hoisting me over his shoulder. I went with a cry, my hands grasping for his black shirt as my feet kicked the air. "Settle down." His huge palm settled on my exposed backside, squeezing my ass. I couldn't take a breath as he swept me from the attic.

Upside down, it was difficult to tell where we were, but I noticed the carpet change as his feet hit the landing. Moments later, he carried me into my bedroom.

"There." He deposited me on the floor, time protracting as his laughter whipped around the space, the ominous sound only intensifying my sense of alarm.

"I need you over here, little girl."

We were moving again, his long strides traveling to the door of my en suite, his fist in my hair ensuring I went with him.

My hands rose to my head in a pathetic attempt to alleviate the fire sparking at my scalp, but it was useless. He dragged me to the door, and by the time I'd assuaged any of the tension, he already had me where he wanted me. I pushed against it. Later, I would think I should have fought him, should have kicked, screamed, and protested in any way possible, but even if that had been a sensible plan, there was no time to counter.

Kade moved so fast, his motion as lithe as his deeds seemed dark, and before I realized what was happening, I was pinned against the door. The hand in my hair shifted to my wrists, tugging the cuffs up and attaching the chain to the hook that sometimes housed my robe. There were two metal pegs attached to the back of my door, and in a heart-beat, I was attached to the highest one, totally helpless to prevent any game Kade wanted to play. Of course, I could have tried to free the cuffs from the metal peg, and in normal circumstances, I liked my chances of achieving that goal, but with Kade pressed up against me, I had no opportunity to struggle. Hell, even my next breath seemed challenging.

"Better." He drew back a couple of inches, sizing me up before his focus flitted to the cuffs. He yanked at one, then the other. "That should hold you while I get things set up, but let's make the view even better, shall we?"

Staring down at me, his lips twitched as his hands fell to the buttons of my nightshirt. I watched in horror as he unfastened the first three, pausing at the fourth and final one.

"Please." I loathed the fear in my voice, wishing I could take it back and transmute it into something with more mettle, but it was pointless pretending. This wasn't a red-hot fantasy from those sites I liked to watch. This was real, and it was happening in my bedroom in my house. I needed to get a grip and fast, or God only knew what this man would do.

"That's lovely, Tiffany." He smiled, one hand rising to prop up my chin and force me to meet his gaze. "Say it again."

My brows knitted at the instruction. "Pl-Please, Master?"

"Mmmm." He ran his tongue over his teeth. "Do you have any idea how hard it makes me when you beg?"

*Oh God.* I swallowed at his question, unsure how on earth I was supposed to answer.

"No."

"Never mind." One black leather shoe moved toward my bare foot, nudging my ankle wider as his fingers concluded with the final button of my shirt. "You'll find out soon enough. Spread those legs for me, little girl."

Widening my stance was the last thing I wanted to do. My shoulders already ached from the awkward position of my arms, but given my current predicament and the unyielding gleam in his eyes, I didn't dare disobey. Heaving in a breath, I inched my right foot farther from the left, praying the limited movement would suffice.

"Come now." He chuckled, tugging at my shirt as if there was anything even vaguely amusing about any of this. "You're going to have to do better than that."

That was the moment I knew—the instance something shifted inside my head. Not that his order was hideous or something debilitating or that it would cause me pain. It was more what the command represented—the reality that he could come in, cuff me to my bathroom door, strip me, and insist I open my legs for him. I snatched in a shaky breath as that thought registered. This wasn't a game, and it wasn't a dream. Kade was there, and his demands were real. He could do whatever the hell he liked.

Holding his gaze, I forced my left ankle to widen, producing space between my thighs.

"Better." His voice oozed with delight. "Now, let me look upon your wonderful body."

Grasping the edge of the shirt, he yanked the two ends of fabric apart, revealing my chest and torso to the cool air and his hungry gaze. "You're just as wonderful as always."

I shivered as he pulled the shirt behind me, compelling the fabric away from my shoulders to display as much of me as possible.

"Naturally, I've had the pleasure of seeing you naked, but this…" He shook his head as if he couldn't believe what was happening. Frankly, I was inclined to agree. "This is something else."

His palms moved toward my body, pawing over my midriff before one rose to my exposed breasts and the other kneaded my ass cheek. I gasped as he manhandled me, frozen with powerlessness. Having fantasized about similar situations for as long as I could recall, my brain was numb to the frantic reality. As his hands moved across my skin, I was aware of my body responding, my nipples budding at his touch and the guttural mewl that escaped my throat, but I couldn't link those deeds to myself. It was as though I was a third party, watching him enjoy my body and unable to tune in or accept the sensations his caresses provoked.

"Fuck, you're lovely." His hand squeezed my ass possessively while the other grazed my other eager nipple. "And so responsive." His face lit up as though I'd done something that deserved a reward. "See, I told you that you'd like what I had in mind."

Kade winked at me as the fingers at my breasts shifted over my bud and pinched hard. I yelled out in pain, but something about the hurt awakened my reactions. Dropped back into my helpless body, I was abruptly conscious of the competing sensations as he skimmed the fingers across my chest and repeated the gesture on my right breast.

"You have amazing tits." Both hands shifted to my bosom, cupping my mounds and clutching them as his gaze seared into me. "Or, should I say, *I* have amazing tits?" His dark laughter echoed around me. "They're going to look great bound and clamped."

"Please!" It was all I could think to say, although I sounded like a broken record.

"You like that idea as well, huh?" He chuckled harder as he leaned down, nuzzling my neck.

"Master." In the end, I resorted to the only word which might placate him.

"I know, I know." His breath was warm at my nape. "I'm being impatient. There'll be time for every decadent thing I want to do to you. Now…" Pulling away, he took a step back, although he still loomed large. "You look sublime, but I must stick to the agenda."

*He had an agenda?* My throat dried at the idea that Kade had every moment planned. Somehow, his insidious scheming made everything seem worse.

"You will stay exactly where I have put you." His finger rose, wagging as if he was instructing a small child. "Don't move or attempt to free yourself, little girl. I promise you I'll make you regret it."

The dark light flaring in his eyes meant I believed him.

"Are we clear?" His question reverberated around the room.

"Y-Yes, Master." I compelled the words from my lips, immobilized by his haunting gray eyes every bit as much as the metal bracelets at my wrists. I'd never seen a gaze like his, so emotive, yet apparently, so cold.

"Good." Swooping, he skimmed his lips over my mouth, taunting me with what I both craved and feared with equal measure. "Keep those wonderful legs spread."

One dark eyebrow arched as his hand fell to my leg, trailing a feathery touch to my sex. I tensed as he neared, knowing I couldn't stop his pursuit. His hand paused at my inner thigh. "I enjoy seeing what belongs to me."

*Fuck.* My eyes fluttered closed as his words rang in my ears. How many books had I read where the alleged hero said something similar? How many erotic scenes had I devoured online?

*He was watching,* my nagging paranoia reminded me. *He*

*already told you. That's how he knows what you want to hear. He's studied you.*

"I also like this." He inched closer as his fingers brushed my labia. His touch was soft and fleeting, but unable to glance down and verify it, I wondered if I'd only imagined the caress. "You wax, is that correct?"

"Yes, Master."

It was easier to speak that time, though heaven only knew why. I was still cuffed and stripped. My future was as uncertain as it was bleak, and I had few reasons to relax.

"I approve," he murmured. "Though I may have to shave you once the hair grows back. I can't exactly take you to the salon like this."

Kade smirked at my dilemma, but his quip sent me into a new spin. If he intended to hold me so long that regrowth was an issue, this was even worse than I'd feared.

"Don't look so scared." He patted my pussy lightly before he turned. "You already know what to do to please me."

Chest rising and falling, I watched him stalk back to the bed. He'd shocked me so far, taking me by surprise and leaving me on the back foot, but if Kade thought he could just tie me up and demand my obedience, he had another think coming.

# CHAPTER 9: KADE

Pacing to her bed, I opened the drawer I knew hid all her favorite sex toys. Glancing up, I took in her stunned expression, relishing her unblinking eyes before my gaze drank in her magnificent body again. Elbows splayed, she looked like one of those hot models from the sites she frequented, all tied up and defenseless as she waited for me to decide her fate. My cock swelled at the alluring thought, and I considered forcing her mouth around its girth.

*No.* I squeezed my eyes closed, insisting the wave of desire pass quickly. I had things to prepare—a plan to stick to. I'd get my pleasure just as soon as everything else was ready. I'd waited this long, hadn't I? I could wait a few more minutes.

Pulling in a deep breath, I smiled at the realization. I'd imagined this moment for so long and could hardly believe how well things were going. So far, Tiffany had barely resisted me, shock aiding my objectives. When I ran my hands over her, she'd reacted with breathy whimpers and desperate gazes. Her responses confirmed what I had come to believe—we were destined to be together. She just didn't know it yet.

"Surprised, little girl?" I didn't bother to suppress my joy as I stared down into the drawer of delights. "You didn't realize I'd found your secret places."

She gulped, nibbling at her lower lip. "No, Master."

"There are many things you don't yet realize." My brow rose as I grasped the items I wanted. "But rest assured, I will enlighten you."

I laid the black ball gag I liked out on the carpet, along with the spreader bar she'd recently purchased. I'd wanted to cheer the night I watched her pull it from its packaging, fingering herself to climax as she played with her new toy. I was thankful to my little girl for having acquired much of the equipment I needed to contain her. Her foresight and attention to detail were welcome.

The sound of metal shifting against metal drew my attention back to my cuffed damsel as she pulled against the cuffs, testing her bondage. Tilting her head, she assessed its confines without moving her legs, her fabulous tits begging for more of my ministrations.

"Not going anywhere, I hope?"

She tensed at my wry tone, her gaze flying back to mine in a heartbeat.

"No, Master." Her reply was immediate.

"I asked you to keep still." I cocked a brow at her, reveling in her short, panicky breaths.

"I-I'm sorry," she panted. "I just wanted to stretch my shoulders, and—"

Lifting one palm, I silenced her attempt at justification. Of course, I understood this was her first time tethered. No doubt she was trying to gauge and understand her own reactions, as well as manage any discomfort, but I couldn't abide disobedience. Even tiny acts of defiance would be quashed with swift discipline. It was the only way she would learn.

"Good girl," I praised as her lips fell silent, though my terse tone did little to convince her of my approval. "Save your breath. I expect compliance. I don't want to hear your excuses."

Pressing her lips into a hard line, her perfect brow creased.

"I'll make sure to reinforce this lesson."

Tiffany's gaze locked with mine, and I could tell she was too terrified to answer. Good, let her fear the potential repercussions. It ought to give her something to ponder while I finished up. She didn't have the final item I sought, so I closed the drawer. Leaving the gag on the floor out of sight, I grasped the spreader bar. I could use the clamps in my pocket to punish her outburst and not have to adjust my plan.

"Recognize this?" I lifted the bar as I wandered to her.

She nodded, her gaze lowering as I neared.

"Words," I demanded. "You may speak."

Christ, it was sexy being able to dictate what she said and when, further proof Tiffany was my living, breathing wet dream. Surely, a woman this perfect was too flawless to slaughter? My lips curled as the thought cemented. Of course, she was. No part of my scheme envisaged extinguishing her glorious light. I intended to keep it burning, heightening its flame with my time and attention.

"Yes, Master."

"What is it?" I waved the bar a few inches from her horrified face. Apparently, she was completely unable to look at her own purchase in my hands.

"A spreader bar."

I sensed how excruciating that was to admit.

"Whose spreader bar, little girl?" I leaned closer, slowing my words as her focus flitted to my face.

"M-Mine, Master."

"That's right." I grinned at the confession. "Since you and everything you have now belong to me, I figure that means it's mine."

She nodded slowly.

"What's it for?"

"Keeping limbs apart," she answered warily.

"Very good." Stroking her heated face with my other hand, I considered kissing her but didn't want to lose sight of my objective—to bind and deride her, whenever possible, using her own equipment. "You enjoyed using it, didn't you?"

She gasped, her eyes as wide as saucers, though she didn't vocalize the obvious question burning in her gaze.

"Yes, I saw," I replied to her unspoken query. "You're a beautiful sight when you make yourself come, but I promise you those orgasms will be even better now that they belong to me."

"Master." Tears pricked her eyes.

"Shhh," I soothed, collecting the first as it raced down her appealing face. "You're doing just fine, and you'll do even better once you're adorned and ready."

Lowering to the floor, I started on her first ankle. I attached the leather cuff around the metal one I'd already placed there and ran the metal bar of the spreader to her other limb. Locking the bar into place, I was reminded of just how slight and delicate the woman was. I would have to go easy if I didn't want to do her actual harm.

"Very nice," I enthused as I rose to my full height. "That will keep those legs where I want them."

"Oh God."

I should have been angry at her frantic plea since I hadn't

given her permission to speak, but the desperation in her voice only turned me on.

"Now, let's try the lower hook, shall we?" I gestured to the metal peg holding her cuffs in place, and reflexively, she tipped her head to follow my gaze. Reaching for her cuffs, I pulled the chain from the highest of the two hooks, sliding it over the lower level. "You should be able to drop to your knees."

I grinned at my plan, signaling for her to obey.

"Master." Her gaze darted between the shackles at her wrists and my face.

"Need help?" I was growing impatient. "Here."

Taking her weight against me, I tipped her forward, forcing her arms to straighten and take the brunt of the strain as I lowered her to her knees before me. She landed gently on the carpet between me and the door, her head now almost at the ideal height for what I had in mind.

"I've seen how good you are with your hands, little girl." I laughed at her mortified expression, catching her falling chin and ensuring she continued to meet my eyes. "Now, you get to show me how good you are with your mouth."

# CHAPTER 10: TIFFANY

My head clouded as he released my chin, my heart pounding faster when his hand rose to his zipper and eased it down. *Oh God.* I'd always known it would come to this—of course, I had. Woken in the night to find myself bound by a ruthless stranger—it was always going to be about his ability to coerce me into whatever course of action he wanted, and Kade hadn't hidden his desire. Kneeling and taking in the enormity of the situation, it was difficult to think.

My instinct to free myself and flee was strong, and fleetingly, I mulled over my earlier opportunities to fight back. I should have taken those, should have offered more resistance.

*Where would that have got you?* My nagging insecurity chided. *He's too strong for you, Tiff. You'd have never won, and you'd probably be in a worse position.*

A worse position? I twisted to glance over my shoulder and took stock of the cuffs holding me in place. Even if I could make it to my feet, I'd struggle to release the metal from the hook without help, and I'd already established there was no easy way to free my wrists from the unyielding bracelets.

"Little girl."

If it was possible, my pulse quickened at his gruff tone.

"Don't look behind you. Look at me."

I lifted my gaze to find his leering face and his hand still loitering at his fly, although he hadn't yet released the organ waiting inside. Pulling in a deep breath, I considered my next steps—what he wanted versus what I was willing and able to give. So far, he'd been reasonably gentle and had only inferred I give head. I could do that, couldn't I? I actually enjoyed oral sex, and if truth be told, I thought Kade was absurdly sexy. Yes, the man was clearly psychotic and had major problems with personal boundaries, but I knew his dark, brooding looks would have turned my head if we'd met on the street.

My eyes fell to where his cock was waiting behind his pants. What was he waiting for? If this was my fate, I might as well relish and revel in the way his touch had liquefied me and give him what he wanted. It wasn't as if I had much choice…

"Know what you have to do, little girl?"

"Yes, Master."

Christ, I sounded eager as he eased his member from the black denim. My brow rose as I took in his girth, the earthy scent of his masculinity wafting past my nostrils as I shifted on my knees.

"Excellent." His hand fell to my left nipple, tugging and tweaking it. "Then I need you to ask like a nice girl."

Wait, what? He wanted me to *ask* for his cock? Was he fucking joking? Yet I couldn't deny the way arousal pooled at the apex of my thighs, his insistence oddly exciting.

"Please, may I have your cock, Master?" It was absurdly easy to ask, and much though I sought to ignore the thrum of arousal it spiked, it goaded me as I batted my lashes at him.

"Yes, you can." His gravelly tone rumbled through me, vibrating straight to my throbbing clit as his hand shifted to the back of my head. "Open up."

My lips parted seconds before he shoved his huge erection past them, and my senses erupted. The essence of Kade filled me up, grazing the back of my throat and overwhelming my taste buds. Tears burned in my eyes as his prick lunged harder, giving me no time to enjoy him. Just like the man himself, this act was destined to be hard and unforgiving, but I couldn't say I disliked it.

I enjoyed the way his hand tightened in my hair, making sure there was nowhere for me to go but to remain open and ready to please him. I liked the utter sense of surrender as I strained against the cuffs and spreader bar. I was, for now at least, *his*—a vessel for his pleasure. The reality taunted as his cock finally relented, withdrawing with a stream of saliva. This was like those dark fantasies I conjured in my head when I wanted to come, similar to the ones I searched for online. The epitome of surrender.

"Open."

Panting, I complied, waiting as he rubbed his pulsing crown around my mouth.

"You are as sexy as fuck like this," he growled. "So pliant and unable to resist me."

Fuck, he was right. This *was* sexy, though it had no right to be—he had no right to treat me this way.

"Lick my balls." Stepping closer, he lifted his shaft and shoved his testicles against my face.

Panting at the change of tack, I strained against his fistful of my hair as I lapped on command. My head fogged with the hedonism. The position—my arms pulled back and my legs permanently parted—was uncomfortable, but the discomfort was easily subdued by my intensifying desire. I wanted him, wanted this, yearned to be used this way. I always had, and while I'd never dreamed a man would be so predatory as to compel me into submission, my body couldn't tell the difference. It responded to his authority the same way it had all those nights I'd slid my fingers into my pussy and imagined capitulation. It craved the surrender.

"Very good," he purred, stroking the back of my neck as he encouraged me forward. "A little girl should lick her master's balls at least once a day. Wouldn't you agree, Tiffany?"

Craning my neck, I tried to make out his face, but squashed against him, it was practically impossible.

"Yes, Master," I just about managed between long laps on his sensitive flesh.

"See how hard you make me?" He yanked me away at the same time he withdrew, his cock strutting out proudly between us.

"Yes, Master." I eyed him, unsure what he'd demand next but knowing I had no choice whatever the answer.

"Now it's time for your punishment."

*Punishment?* My brow furrowed as he delved into his right pocket.

"Your penance for moving when I asked you to be still and trying to explain your disobedience when you should have remained quiet."

"I…" I started to speak, but the intensity of his stare silenced me. There was nothing I could say, nothing to be said. I just wanted to revel in his moment and pray to God I woke up safely in my bed to find this was all only a sordid dream.

"Smart girl." His smirk should have riled, but burgeoning arousal laced with my fear ensured compliance. "You don't want to upset your master any more." Reaching into his pocket, he pulled something free. "Know what these are?" His palm opened, my gaze devouring the small metal clips on his hand.

"Oh God." My throat dried as I absorbed my fate. "Nipple clamps."

"That's right." His smile widened, and I noticed his cock pulsed as he collected one of the clamps between his thumb and forefinger. "I know you like them. I've seen your internet search history, remember."

I gasped, dread mushrooming as I imagined how much the clamps would bite. "I've never actually used them. I don't think I'll be able to—"

His long index finger pressed into my lips, halting my sentence.

"You'll be able to."

His voice was absurdly soothing, considering he was the captor who'd been hiding away in my attic, biding his time and waiting to pounce. There should have been nothing reassuring about his presence, nothing alluring about his touch, yet I found solace in the light caress of his fingertip. I sensed what I would never be brave enough to say aloud—I wanted him. I'd craved the touch of a man like Kade for most of my adult life.

Craning my head to meet his silver-blue gaze, my every fiber focused on what he would do next. Would the clamps hurt as much as I assumed they would, or—even more terrifyingly—would I be drawn to their relentless pressure, just as I was called to the man exerting it?

"You'll wear them for me while I enjoy your mouth." His

finger slid to my chin, insisting my attention never left his face. "And for as long as I say after."

Christ, had anyone ever made anything sound as sexy as Kade did?

"If you're a good girl and wear them for me without a fuss, I might reward you."

*Reward me?* What the fuck did that mean? So far, I'd woken up and had been accosted by a complete stranger. A reward might be him leaving me the hell alone, but perturbingly, I couldn't even say hand on heart that was what I wanted.

Kade was the living embodiment of my fantasies, as though the antiheroes from the paperbacks I devoured had come to life and captured me. He was more than I could have imagined, and right now, he was waving nipple clamps in front of my eyes.

"You want to be rewarded, don't you?" His taunting tone washed over, and I answered without thinking.

"Yes, Master."

"Good," he growled, releasing my chin and lowering to his haunches in front of me. "Then you must learn to take your punishment."

Fighting for air as the clamps neared, my nipples lengthened at his touch in preparation. I should have been thankful he was taking the time to ready me for the pain, but God help me, as his strong fingers tweaked and pinched my sensitive buds, all I could think was how good it felt, how right —*this* was what I'd been waiting for. Barely acknowledging the ache in my knees and shoulders, I could only think about Kade's will and where it would lead me.

Dropping one clamp, his concentration settled on my left breast. I held my breath as he drew back the tiny metal arms.

"This is going to hurt." He closed the arms around my

bud, eyeing me as I cried out. I tried to process the new sensation, closing my eyes as the metal pinched my teat.

"Good," he cooed, his voice drawing my gaze open. The contorted ball of energy in my belly tightened as I realized he actually had the audacity to grin as he set to work on my right nipple. "You took that well, Tiffany."

*Oh God.* I kept the words in this time, concentrating on each breath as he clamped the metal to my other bud. *Oh God, this was too much.* How would I bear this? How could I tolerate the intensity for more than a few minutes?

"I'm impressed."

Kade gave me little time to dwell on my despair, rising to his full height and grazing his engorged erection over my face. My suffering turned him on every bit as much as the bondage thrilled me. There was little doubt—we were both mad.

"I thought you'd cry and beg, but you're more stoic than I gave you credit for."

I shifted on my knees, my eyes falling closed as he skimmed precum across my cheek. It was denigrating to be objectified—to become a thing he could use and torment however he liked—but then, that was the point. Kade seemed to know I reveled in these desires. He knew about the websites I watched and deleted from my browser, knew where I kept my sex toys, and worse, he seemed to know which of my buttons to push.

"Open your eyes." His voice lowered to a snarl, compelling obedience. "I want to see the pain in them."

"Kade." His name stuck in my throat, barely a whisper, as his hand shifted to my throat.

"What was that?"

"M-Master." I forced the word out, aware of his hand tightening on my windpipe.

"I'm going to fuck your mouth." He never broke eye contact, and tension ratcheted in my body as I consciously tried to disregard the biting metal on my nipples and relieve some of the tension in my shoulders. "Remember, this is a punishment. I'm not interested in your pleasure, only your compliance."

His cock lunged into my mouth, splintering all rational thought as it hit the back of my throat. My instinct to gag was tempered by his hand, still lingering on my neck like an omnipresent threat as he thrust over and over.

I could scarcely even think as he fucked my mouth, tears burning in my eyes as he used me. In the depths of my desires, I'd dreamed of being taken this way, manhandled and treated roughly, but none of the self-love had prepared me for the reality—the overwhelming sense of panic as I struggled for breath and the incredible feeling of powerlessness. It was horrific, yet beneath the layers of alarm, it was something else as well. My body responded to his dominance, to the very real impetus of his huge hands, enormous prick, and the unyielding clamps. This time I was truly fucked.

"Yes," he snarled. "You are magnificent."

Pulling his cock away, his fingers rose from my neck to my hair. Burying them into its depths, he wrenched my head back in time to catch the first remnants of his pleasure. I gasped for air, the fire lighting at my scalp worth the agony if it meant I could breathe again.

"Keep that mouth open." His growl reverberated as he pumped another round of cum over me. Complying as best I could, my eyes fluttered closed as I captured it between my lips, surrendering to his will.

"Yes." His fingers tightened, but I didn't move. I didn't want to upset the balance between us. He'd found his high, so maybe he'd be more lenient and willing to listen. Maybe he'd let me go and chalk this up to experience? Though as he wiped the remainder of his orgasm over my chin, I knew that was a ridiculous hope.

The woman, bound and clamped on her knees, had no chance.

# CHAPTER 11: KADE

"You survived, little girl." I glowered at her panting form, waiting as tear-stained eyes met mine. My lips twitched at how wonderful she looked, gratified the trembling mess on the carpet was all my doing. "How are those clamps?"

Her blue eyes flickered as if she couldn't believe I was asking. Frankly, she had a good point. I didn't know why I was suddenly so concerned with her welfare, but the oddest part was I genuinely cared. I would take Tiffany as my own and do with her whatever I chose, but that didn't mean I wanted to damage her. She was as precious as the orchids I'd had delivered, more beautiful and fragile and completely unable to exist without my attention.

"They hurt, Master." She heaved in a breath. "A lot."

"Excellent." I could hardly suppress the glee in my voice. "Then they've done the job I required."

"Please."

Despite my recent climax—the first of a great many, I intended to have with her—my balls clenched at her breathy plea.

"Please, Master."

"You need them to come off?"

God, it was glorious, toying with her. The clamps would be removed when I decided, but witnessing her beg was even more fucking delightful than I'd imagined—and I *had* imagined.

"Yes, please." Her gaze flitted to mine frantically. "I'll be good, I promise."

"Oh, I know you will."

Slipping my cock away, I fell to my knees. There was little doubt her arms and shoulders had to be in agony, and the spreader was doing a fine job of making sure she couldn't close her legs. Whatever I decided, she would need to change position soon, but for now, the clamps could remain. My hands grazed over her breast, causing her breathing to spike.

"But first, I'm going to move you."

Tiffany should be careful about the promises she made. I would ensure they came back to bite worse than even the clamps. She panted in response, biting her lip as if she was swallowing back her retort.

*Good.* I rose, tracing an invisible line past her shoulders and up to the cuffs. Let her hold in the snarky comments, which would only land her in more hot water.

"I'll need you to straighten up."

"I-I don't know if I can, Master."

Christ, she sounded deliciously desperate.

"My weight is pushed forward, and my knees are killing me."

"Fine." Pressing my palm into her chest, I eased her backward, rolling my eyes at her yelp. So much for the stoicism she'd shown earlier. A few minutes with the clamps seemed to have obliterated it altogether. "Up you come."

I didn't bother asking for her help this time. Snaking an

arm around her waist, I hiked her to her feet, settling her swaying body before finally lifting the cuffs from the bathroom hook. I eyed it gratefully, acknowledging what a sound job it had done, teaching my little girl her first important lesson. She mewled as I eased her arms down and completed my circuit back to my original position.

"You were a good girl."

My voice revealed none of my conviction. I had no urge to lessen my grip on the terrified woman. I'd worked so hard to get to this point, to see her tethered and at my mercy, and even though I would offer her the reward I'd dangled, I didn't want her to think things would be easy from now on. That was far from the truth.

"Guess what you're getting in return?"

Her chin lifted, confusion flickering past the agony in her eyes.

"I don't know, Master."

"Yes, you do." Buoyed by her apparent willingness to cede, I smiled. "It's what you always want when you creep up here to your bedroom." My smile grew as embarrassment burned in her cheeks. "What you seek when you trawl the internet for satisfaction."

Betrayal flashed in those beautiful watery eyes when they finally relented and met mine, a different hurt from the biting clamps. So, she didn't like that I knew her private business? That was a shame because, as Miss Noble was about to discover, that was only the tip of the iceberg. Kade Walker knew *everything*.

"What is it?"

She flustered at my question, and I drank in the sight of her, exposed and powerless to prevent the metal from pinching her fabulous assets.

"Pleasure?" Her brow furrowed as if she wasn't sure of

her answer, but on this one point, little Tiffany had nothing to worry about.

"Yes, little girl… pleasure." I held her gaze for a long moment before seizing her lips, forcing her to open and let me in. She ceded with a groan, leaning into me as my tongue explored her heat. Inside my pants, my cock stirred once more, imagining the other hot, wet places it could fill.

"I will keep you as my captive." I drew away, searing her with my gaze. "And you, little girl, will do everything I ask of you." Her chest rose and fell between us, the edges of the clamps grazing across the fabric of my clothing. "When you do my bidding, you'll be rewarded with pleasure of your own."

Her pupils dilated, and her lids fluttered as she registered my instructions.

"That's how it will be."

"Master."

My erection strained to be free, the resonance of her plea speaking directly to the organ.

"Hmmm?"

"I'm scared."

My lips curled at her confession. "I know." I wouldn't deny what an aphrodisiac that was. "But that's not all you feel, is it?" My hand rose to her hair, fisting it until her eyes flickered open. "Is it?"

"N-No."

"Tell me what else." I wanted to kiss her again, to run my hands all over her body and make her mine entirely. "Tell me what you feel."

Her mouth parted, but only a strangled mewl escaped.

"Tiff-any." I arched a dissatisfied eyebrow at her. "Tell. Me."

"Horny." She swallowed, her expression portraying her panic, yet still, she repeated it. "I feel horny, Master."

"Very good." A flicker of genuine pride bloomed in my chest. Tiffany was the one part of my scheme I couldn't account for. I could plan every other moment and make sure everything was where it should be, but I could never second-guess her reactions. She might have crumpled at the first sight of capture, or she might have fought. I had no way of knowing. In the end, she'd taken a more satisfying third way.

"Hands behind your back. I'll see for myself."

I eased the nightshirt from her body before she complied as much as the cuffs allowed, revealing her magnificence as I wandered behind her. Taking my time, I made her wait as I loomed over her, and as I pressed closer, her fidgety fingers brushed over the growing bulge in my trousers.

"Let me see what you've made of your punishment."

Gathering her beautiful hair away from her right shoulder, I nuzzled her soft skin, nipping her nape as my hands traveled around her body, one settling at her hip, holding her close, while the other slipped between her legs. She was wonderfully smooth as my fingers paused at her labia.

"I've wanted to do this so many times."

For once, I didn't want the confession to frighten her. I only wanted to share the brimming passion that burgeoned and let her know how she affected me. This wasn't all about exerting power, about the fact she was weak, while I was strong, a woman where I was a man. It was about something far more compelling, a call that drew me to her months ago, a connection I couldn't dismiss.

"Oh." Her voice was a hoarse whisper as she leaned into the crook of my neck. If there was fear lurking inside her mind, she wasn't letting it show.

Brushing one fingertip over her clit, I grinned when her hips jerked forward. It was impossible for her legs to close, a fact I hoped would heighten her excitement and hinder her escape.

"What does my little girl need?"

There was no need to tease her, but fuck knows, it was endlessly amusing, and since this was the first opportunity to actually touch and taste my prize, I intended to revel in the moment. I longed to hear passion from her lips, craved the acknowledgment that despite my morally gray advance, she yearned for me every inch as much as I wanted her.

"You." Her voice broke, her breath ragged as if the divulgence was too much for her to bear.

"Ask me properly." I pressed my lips to her neck, trailing the hand at her hip to her clamped tit. Cradling her firm breast, I breathed in all of her wonders as my finger circled her swollen ball of nerves. "Tell your master what you would like." Lifting my head, I caught sight of her nibbling at her lip, her senses clearly frazzled by the competing sensations.

"Please, Master."

The words seemed to come more easily.

"What?" I urged, sliding another digit between her lips to find out for myself just how my treatment had been received. Predictably, Tiffany hadn't let me down. Her sex was flooded with arousal. "What do you need?"

"To come, please." Pressure mounted in her tone, begging me to see reason and do what I'd promised—enough to take her there—anything. *Something.*

"Oh, baby." She was driving me wild with her frantic breathy noises, my already swollen organ desperate to be where my hand was.

"Like this?" I pushed two fingers inside her pussy, taking

her weight when her knees buckled. Twisting my palm, I grazed her needy clit as I pumped my digits in and out of her sex.

"Yes," she gasped, struggling for her breath as her hips pushed forward, seeking more depth.

"Greedy, little girl," I admonished with a chuckle. "You will learn to take what you are given."

"Y-Yes, Master." Her lips parted as I increased the pace, her body immobilized with the impending pleasure. Watching her ascension, my other hand slid to her nipple and tugged at her clamped tissue.

"Oh, fuck!" she hissed, writhing in my embrace.

"Now, now, now," I chastised, loving her responses. "Your master doesn't want that sort of language from his little girl."

"I'm sorry, but—" Her sentence was cut short as I withdrew from her scintillating cunt and smacked her clit. "Oh, yes!"

"Oh, you like that?" Tiffany was growing more and more enticing by the second.

"I don't know." She sounded weary with the passion. "Please."

"I'll help you," I assured her. "But you get pain with your pleasure, little girl. That's the deal."

"Oh God!" Squirming in my arms, her back arched and her ass teased my arousal.

"Get back in position," I growled, my tone insisting on her cooperation.

Finding her clit again, I circled the hungry nub before slipping my fingers back into her warm pussy and fucking her. Slow, firm, demanding strokes claimed her, holding her captive every inch as much as the metal encasing her limbs. Pressing my palm against her clit, I surveyed her need, enjoying the way her hips rocked forward and back. She was close. Despite the fear and concern I'd inspired, I was going to tear this orgasm from her and cement what would soon be obvious.

*Tiffany was mine.*

# CHAPTER 12: TIFFANY

Lost to his rhythm, I was in a frenzy of desire. Ecstatic as his fingers filled me, energized when he smacked my desperate clit, and even unconsciously willing him to play with the clamps at my nipples. Yes, I knew it would hurt like hell, but for some messed-up reason, there was something to his theory. Each time he ramped up the passion, edging me back to the brink of utopia, the pain would sweep through my brain, taking my breath away. I lurched from one sensation to the next, only aware the timing and decision were his. Unable to resist, there was nothing I could do to halt his progress, but God help me, I didn't care to.

I craved his caress, blooming at the heat of his breath on my neck, and beyond anything else, as he intensified the pleasure, I was ready to come apart. I needed it; deserved that much for everything he had put me through.

"Ready to come?"

Oh God, I was more than ready.

"Yes, Master." My hips jerked with each slap of my needy

bud, the wet sounds of my arousal inspiring only hedonism where they should have provoked shame.

"Does this greedy little clit want the pleasure?"

Imagining his fingers lurking over the clamps, ready to torment me further, I refused to open my eyes and discover for myself. I sensed his swelling erection at my ass, hoping to bury itself into me through his pants.

"Yes, Master."

"I always knew you were a greedy girl." He chuckled, quickening the pace of his spanks. Each strike jolted through me, electrifying my clit and amplifying my need. I'd never known anything as glorious or as consuming. "But this is something special."

"Oh!" I whimpered, my pussy clenching at his heightening power. I couldn't do anything without his permission—couldn't stop him, couldn't get away, couldn't come.

"Come for me now, and afterward, you will thank me." His voice sounded distant, but from some far-off place, his words echoed. "Understand?"

"Yes, Master." I would have agreed to anything if it meant he didn't stop. He could never stop.

"Good."

His swats built, one sweet strike after the next until my clit was pounded by the direct stimulation. Tension peaked in my body, and I screamed as the orgasm I craved finally ripped through me.

A few seconds into my fervor, my eyes flew open, pain erupting first from my left, then my right nipple. I folded into his arms, vaguely aware of the evil clamps hitting the ground. Distraught at the ache I couldn't rub better, I was trapped by the pinnacle of my lust.

"Fabulous." His voice was smooth, like a stiff drink when you needed one. "And?"

Forcing my brain into gear, I strained to recall his latest demand.

"Thank you, Master."

My response was almost a sigh, and bizarrely, I actually meant it. I'd never been so terrified, never been treated so disrespectfully, yet as his cum dried on my face and his fingers slid into my soaking wet sex, I was forced to accept what was patently clear.

Sex might never be this good again.

"You did very well." His words vibrated over me as his digits eased in and out—taunting me with the prospect of more pleasure. "I knew you would."

Leaning into his body, I groaned, no longer knowing what I wanted. Now that he'd taken me to the edge of heaven, did I want more? Or did I just want to lay my head on my pillow, wake up, and discover this was all just one salacious dream? The question goaded.

"Tired, little girl?"

Was I? I couldn't even put my emotions into words anymore.

"Yes, Master." I closed my eyes, letting go of whatever shame surfaced at the title. I was doing what I had to do to survive. I didn't *like* ceding to him. This wasn't my choice. My toes curled at the half-lie.

"Time for bed then."

I yelped as he swept me off my feet, my eyes flying open as I landed on the bed to find him towering over me.

"I'm going to release the cuffs." Kade arched a dark eyebrow. "If I get so much as a flicker of resistance from you, I'll make sure you don't sleep a wink tonight."

My heart raced, unsure whether the adrenaline was fueled by fear or twisted arousal.

"Got it?"

His voice thundered around the master bedroom, and fleetingly, I wondered if my neighbor, Natalie, would hear him. I hadn't gotten to know her, or anyone in the neighborhood, that well, but she knew I was single. A booming male voice in the middle of the night was not a normal occurrence.

"Yes." I pulled in a breath, conscious of how vulnerable I was. I wanted out of the cuffs, and I'd do whatever I had to do to expedite my release.

Nodding, he reached into his pocket, though his gaze never left mine.

"Remember what I said." He walked to my side, lowering slowly before tugging at my wrists. "You have a beautiful home, little girl."

Wait, what? He was making small talk while he unfastened the bondage?

"Th-Thank you, Master." I didn't know what else to say.

"I've enjoyed being here."

A shiver of horror raced along my spine at the reminder that Kade had been here, lurking in the shadows of my house for God only knew how long. It was such an intrusion.

"There."

The bracelets around my wrists fell away, and I wanted to cry with relief.

"Hands by your side." Flicking the cuffs into the air and catching them again, he came to stand in front of me. "Get in bed."

I glanced back at my pillow, the lace I'd happily gone to sleep on only a few hours ago. What did this command mean? He couldn't seriously expect me to just go back to sleep? I doubted I'd ever feel safe in the house again.

"Why am I waiting, little girl?"

I scrambled across the duvet as quickly as my limbs would coordinate, slipping under the cover.

"Your arms need a rest."

He was talking to himself as he strode around the bed to join me, his attention falling to the carpet. Brows knitting, I glanced at the half-open drawer to find a selection of sex toys on display, heat blooming in my face, recognizing them as mine. My breathing accelerated. How long had he been here, looking through my things and watching me? This was so wrong, yet the way he'd played my body had been electrifying. How could I reconcile the competing emotions?

"Stretch out."

He rose to his full height, those smoldering gray eyes burning into my skin as I complied. I didn't trust him, didn't want to give away what little liberty the cuffs had gifted, but what choice did I have? Kade was huge, strong, and incredibly intimidating, as well as possibly the sexiest guy I'd ever seen.

"I'll use this so you can get some sleep."

Lifting his enormous hands into view, he stretched the black leather between his fingers, his smirk growing in my peripheral vision. There was no need to ask what it was. I'd seen them many times on online videos, as well as at the pet store.

"Do you like it?" His tone oozed condescension. "I chose it for you."

He chose it?

"It's a collar." My throat dried with the answer, my eyes widening as he leaned closer.

"Answer the question, little girl." His voice deepened. "You do not wanna piss me off."

"I like it." Alarm ballooned at his menacing growl.

"I thought you might." He grinned, dropping it onto my belly. "Put it on."

*What?* He wanted me to put the damn thing on? Was he insane?

"Yes." His jaw stiffened. "I want you to put it on, and I do not appreciate being made to wait."

Grabbing the leather, I wrapped it around my neck, fumbling with the buckle. My chest rose and fell under his supervision, and a desperate whimper escaped my throat before I finally secured the metal at my throat. What had I done? It was one thing to be coerced into behavior, but this was crazy—I'd actually put the collar on myself!

"Hands down." He batted my fingers away as his digits moved in to check my handiwork. Tugging at the leather, he slipped a finger under it and forced me toward him. "Just checking that you've left yourself enough room to breathe, little girl." His lips twitched, my pulse quickening at the sinister gesture. "I wouldn't want you running out of oxygen."

# CHAPTER 13: KADE

Tiffany looked shell-shocked as I reached for the chain I'd purchased. Online shopping meant I'd been able to buy everything she didn't already have, and now, I had both the time and opportunity to try them out.

"Get back down." I encouraged her back to bed, enjoying the weight of her delicious tit in my palm as she relented. The teat had been crushed by the unforgiving clamp, but her soft skin wasn't damaged. "Arms by your side."

I sensed her reluctance as she forced her limbs into position. The minx was used to pleasuring herself at the idea of obedience, but the reality was more of an effort. I smiled at the amusing thought, not that it mattered. I was officially in her life, and everything she'd ever known would change from this point on. Her feelings on the subject were as irrelevant as the weather.

"Good." Opening the metal clip at the end of the chain, I secured it to the D-ring at the front of her collar.

"Oh, no," she panted, her expression pained as she

watched me tug the chain to her bedstead and wind it around the wood.

"Hush." My terse tone more than conveyed my displeasure. I didn't expect her to speak unless she was spoken to. Tiffany was beautiful and thoroughly entertaining, but her independent streak grated. With time and patience, she would be trained to my liking. Fortunately for us both, I was usually a patient man.

"Why are you doing this, Master?"

She rolled frantically to one side as I finished tethering her to the bed. Following her impromptu lead, I pushed her onto her belly. Pulling the blanket down, I smacked her delightful ass, relishing the reverberation echoing across her skin. Christ, the woman had a bottom made for my palm. The sweet realization goaded me into another fast flurry of swats.

"Ouch!" she cried, attempting to scramble up the bed.

"Oh, no." I laughed, tugging her hips back to the mattress and pressing down with my free palm. "You stay right here and get spanked."

"But—" She lifted her chin, trying to argue, but was silenced as my palm peppered her flesh. "Please!" Struggling, her hands slid to her ass as if she could fend off my advances, but I captured her tiny limbs, holding them into the small of her back as I chastised her. The noise of each impact furled with the sumptuous sight of her submission—a heady demonstration of my every lurid fantasy—until her cheeks were a wonderful rosy hue, and my cock was ready to claim her properly.

"I'll spank you when I choose to." Excitement soared as I declared my new freedoms out loud. "I use you when I want to, and you, little girl, have no say."

She turned her face toward me, revealing large, frightened eyes.

"We both know this is what you want." I licked my lips, hardly believing how well my plan had morphed into real life. I'd chosen the middle of the night on purpose, wanting Tiffany to be drowsy and malleable, but I never expected to force my first orgasm from her so soon. Now, chained to the bed with an adorable spanked behind, she was truly mine for the taking. "There's no point denying it." I squeezed her right cheek, chuckling at her agitated mewl. "I can give you everything you've ever desired, little girl."

Her brow furrowed, mistrust flickering in her enthralling eyes. *What do you know about my desires?* The question never made her lips because she knew better. Tiffany realized her insolence would only earn her more punishment, and more fundamentally, I hoped she understood the answer all too well. After so long surveying her, fathoming her needs and routines, I *did* know her. I knew what made her tick and what would set her on fire, and I would use both against her.

"An entire world of surrender and lust." Dipping my fingers, I grazed a line over her wet cunt as my other hand held her wrists steady. "More pleasure than you can stand."

"Why?" Her voice was hardly even a whisper.

"Wrong answer." Lifting my hand, I smacked her ass hard, relishing the way she gasped at the sting. "You say, *thank you, Master.*"

Her eyes were filled with tears when her gaze fixed on me again.

"Thank you, Master." She was exhausted and utterly stunned by my aggressive approach. That was pleasing. If my ego was allowed to dictate the terms, I might have also said she was broken, but I wasn't a fool. I knew better. A woman as intelligent as Tiffany wouldn't break so easily. I had to be prepared for the long fight.

"I can give you everything." I relaxed, slipping my hand back between her legs. "I can satisfy all those fantasies you're too ashamed to tell anyone about. The ones you read about, the ones you watch while you finger fuck yourself." My smile grew as her blush deepened. "Trust me, I'm the one, Tiffany. I already know about them, already know what you need."

She squirmed under my hands, her toes curling as she tried, and failed, to close her legs and halt my exploration.

"All of this can be yours, little girl, and all you have to do is give me one thing in return."

Panting, she heaved in a breath. "What?"

Swatting her pussy, my balls tightened at the expression of pain on her face. Leaning close, I growled the words into her ear.

"Every. Single. Part. Of. You."

# CHAPTER 14: TIFFANY

Shock was peculiar. It must have been at least an hour since I'd stirred in the attic and this warped turmoil had started. An hour of dread and panic, fused with the most delicious hedonism—an hour to get my bearings and start the makings of a plan of resistance, but it was only now that everything fell into place. His words resounded in my head, squeezing my airway closed as if the leather at my neck had shrunk and stolen my oxygen.

*Every. Single. Part. Of. You.*

That's what he sought—to devour and own all of me, and sprawled out, fettered, and pinioned by his weight, it was difficult to see how I could stop him.

"Ready to do as you're told?"

His hot breath warmed my arm, his hand still pushing my palms into my back. If only I was strong enough to free myself, I could get this bloody collar off, and surely, I'd be able to tackle the spreader bar, but there was no hope of that, no point even contemplating it. Kade was too tough, able to placate me with only his hand. I had no chance of escaping him—not now, not like this.

"Please." I turned my face, mumbling into my pillow as I heaved in a breath. No longer knowing what I was pleading for, my weariness at the long days and unsatisfying nights bled into my desperation until my every fiber was full of self-pity.

"Little girl."

I tensed at his gruff tone, compelling my concentration back in his direction.

"You need to sleep, and I need silence." He knelt at the side of the bed, lips curling as he gazed down at my no-doubt petrified face. "Are we clear?"

I nodded, not knowing what else to do but knowing for damn certain I wouldn't sleep in my current predicament.

"Thinking you won't sleep like that?" He tilted his head, apparently amused, but my head splintered into a thousand pieces.

*How?* How did he always seem to know what I was thinking? It was bad enough that the man had been lurking around my home for God knew how long, hiding and watching me, but it seemed as if he'd crept inside my head as well.

"No need to worry." He lessened his grip on my wrists, patting my ass playfully. "I'm going to help you, Tiffany. I'm always here to help you."

*Oh God.* The words screamed in my head, though I was too scared to vocalize them. Kade had never clarified what he would do if I pushed the boundaries too far and displeased him, and I wasn't in a hurry to find out.

"Roll onto your back."

His weight disappeared, leaving me free, aside from the collar at my neck and the bar between my ankles. Pulling in hot ribbons of air, I steeled myself, turning as he requested.

"You are fucking lovely." His eyes shone as he devoured

the sight of my chest and belly. "To show I've been thinking about you, I had this moment all prepared." Chuckling, he lifted the mattress, sending me rolling into the center of the bed with a squeal. "Careful."

I could hear the glee in his voice as one hand caught me, steadying me until he lowered the thing. Breath ragged, I met his eyes. What the fuck was he doing?

"Here." He held up a black strap as if he was once again answering my silent question.

My brow creased as I took in the sight of it. What was that? Before I had time to figure out the riddle, he reached for my right arm, slid my hand into what looked like a pre-prepared loop, and tightened the material until it knotted at my wrist.

*Shit!* I stared at my wrist in disbelief, as if anything about this latest bondage was confusing compared to what he'd accomplished already.

"You're gonna be just fine."

Locking gazes with me for the longest second, Kade leaped lithely onto the bed, over the cover, and landed on his feet before I could draw another breath.

"No!" The strangled word caught in my throat as I watched him repeat the process on the other side of the bed, time moving in slow motion as this time, he pulled a long length of a strap from under my mattress.

*How had that got there?* The question ricocheted in my mind, demanding an answer. When the hell had he readied my bed for this chaos? How had I been so blind that I had noticed nothing about his intrusion? Christ, he must have been here in my bedroom... *in my bed.* I panted harder at the perturbing thought.

By the time he'd captured my left wrist, I was sitting up

again, straining against the chains and straps keeping me in place.

"Uh-oh." He fought my left arm into submission, ignoring my screams as he wrangled the knot into position. "Don't fight me, little girl. I promise you won't win."

"Please!"

I was like a machine, a constant flurry of throaty pleads I couldn't control. Pulling against the new binds at my wrists, I couldn't believe I hadn't done more to resist, to stop him from taking this final semblance of control, but what could I have done? Piece by piece, Kade had dismantled any chance of escape.

"Last chance to settle down." He shook his head as he climbed from the bed, though his curling lips conveyed more amusement than displeasure. Rattled, I couldn't decide which was the most vexing. "Be quiet and make this easier on yourself."

Crossing my bedroom, he sunk to his knees at the side of the bed, my belly knotting as he studied what was left of the paraphernalia he selected earlier.

"Did I ask you to sit up?" He didn't even look my way as he asked, but lowering to my back, I knew I didn't want to see whatever expression his handsome face wore. "Better."

I stared at the ceiling, half terrified and half distraught at my performance. I couldn't want this, *didn't* want this, so why wasn't I fighting harder?

"I know it's late." He climbed to his feet, my eyes straining to see what he'd chosen, though he held it behind his back, teasing me. "I know you're scared, but I will not accept your willful disobedience." Storm clouds gathered in his eyes as he admonished.

"I'm sorry." I wasn't sorry in the slightest, but the growing air of alarm he created was making it difficult to think.

"What was that?" he snapped, leaning over me.

"Master." I met his eyes, completely at his mercy and horrified at what might come next.

"One day, you'll realize what a kind and generous master I am."

He brought his hand from behind his back, revealing my most recent acquisition and a roll of bondage tape to my astonished eyes. The slim, sleek black vibrator had only arrived last month, and it had already brought me to repeated soul-shattering climaxes.

*What are you going to do?* My eyes thundered the question my lips dared not speak, though as his hand lowered to my sex, everything became clearer.

"Nothing makes me sleepier than an orgasm." He turned toward me, one eyebrow arching as he placed the plastic at my labia. "Wouldn't you agree?"

Was he actually inviting me to speak? Lips parted, I watched as he ripped a length of tape from the roll and used it to secure the vibrator in place. I jerked as the device skimmed my clit, knowing only too well how easily it could push me over the precipice, even when Kade hadn't already taken me there.

"Ready?" His smile was predatory, conveying nothing of the apparent pleasure he was giving. "You may answer."

Suddenly, my throat was dry. "I-I don't understand, Master." Why was he prepared to give me more pleasure if he wanted me to sleep? Why was he doing any of this?

"You will." His grin was far from reassuring, and a moment later, he flicked the power on, whirring my toy into life.

Arching at the buzzing sensation, aware of its vicinity to my clit, I was already desperate for its help. I didn't know what Kade was doing, but if his idea of sleep was giving me more pleasure, I would take it. Better pleasure than pain, right? Better his smile, then his sneer. I needed the man on my side if I was to have any hope of making it out of this ordeal alive.

"Look at you." Chuckling, he reached into his pocket and pulled out his phone, waving it in front of me. "Fucking magnificent."

"Oh God."

My orgasm was already close, my hips rising to encourage the end of the vibrator to graze my needy bud. I wanted this. I had no idea why and would never be able to explain it to another living soul, but in this moment of frenzied feeling, I only recognized the truth. I craved the pleasure, just as much as I'd longed for it all those long evenings I'd sat in front of my laptop and let my imagination topple me into titillation. It seemed as though Kade had been sent here to deliver it for me.

"Yes," he enthused, reaching to shift the pulsing device. "Just a little more to the clit, I think."

I groaned as soon as the plastic made contact, aware of the binds at my wrist and neck—the very first time my burning fantasies had been brought to life.

"That's better."

I closed my eyes at his smug tone, blocking him out, only wanting to focus on the high. I didn't know what would happen beyond this moment, this climax, the next gasping breath, but as crazy as it sounded, I didn't care. Let the cards fall as they may. I would take the pleasure just as I had been forced to accept the fear.

"Look at me."

Jarred by his order, it took a few seconds for me to realize what he was actually doing with his phone. My eyes widened as I registered he was recording the scene, stroking his swollen cock as he enjoyed the look of me.

*Oh God! Oh God, no!* The swell of arousal I'd been reveling in subsided as I struggled in my tethers. This was beyond humiliating. It was awful enough to be bound and treated this way by a complete stranger, but to know he was preserving the moment for prosperity was horrific. I had to get hold of that phone, had to get—

"Thank your master for this pleasure." His order broke my train of thought.

What pleasure? I hadn't even gotten to the pleasure yet.

"Th-Thank you, Master." I eyed the vibrator frantically, torn between my desire for another orgasm and the disgust Kade's actions inspired. Did I want it to go on and topple me, or if I could, would I rip the damn thing away and shove it down his throat?

"Good, little girl."

I clenched as he brought the phone nearer, concentrating on my sex.

"Look how fucking wet you are."

Oh fuck, he was right. I *was* wet, his earlier ministrations and the incessant whir of my vibrator had seen to that, but my body's responses didn't justify his behavior. How could he think this was right? How was it okay to go into someone's house, tie them up, and record their plight? How could anyone think that was acceptable?

"Oh, yes." I didn't know what I was asking for as I tried to catch my breath. I only knew the competing heightening emotions were making it difficult to think about anything except the pulsing plastic at my pussy.

"Wonderful." Dropping his phone onto the bed between my legs, he leaned closer, stroking my labia. "Don't fight it, little girl. Let the pleasure wash you away."

# CHAPTER 15: KADE

Tiffany's body tensed, her long limbs stiff as she called out. "Oh God!" Anguish swept through her tone, her gasping breaths and curling toes an indication of the intensity. I captured it all on my phone—videos I would enjoy time and time again.

"Beautiful," I purred appreciatively. "How many was that, little girl?"

A throaty mewl escaped her parting lips before she could form words, a response to the incessant whirr of the device and its unrelenting vibration ready to take her right back to the edge with deft efficiency.

"F-Four." She was hoarse, her eyes fluttering closed as if the number was an admission of guilt.

"Sorry?" Reaching for her tempting chest, I pinched the nearest nipple hard. Her body arched at the contact, her cries growing louder.

"Master!"

"You have to get better at remembering," I admonished. "Once you're rested, I will punish you every time you forget." I couldn't fucking wait.

"Y-Yes, Master."

Releasing her nipple, I assessed her flushed face. How long could I keep driving her to and from the brink before she lost consciousness? It would be fun finding out.

"Feeling sleepy yet?" My tone was sardonic, though I sensed its wry quality was lost on the woman writhing on the bed in front of me.

"Please." A singular tear escaped down her cheek when her eyes squeezed closed. "No more."

"Don't be silly." I was having way too much fun to stop. Tiffany might not realize it yet, but I'd been planning this for a lifetime. There was no chance I would yield to pathetic unsolicited pleas. "We're not even close to stopping."

"But Master." Her hips rose, and she moaned as if the movement was agony. "I can't take anymore."

"Then you must learn." Reaching between her legs, I skimmed a digit along the edge of the plastic, smiling at the moisture collected on my fingertip. Tiffany was making it easy—by the time the whirring device had done its job, she'd be drenched with desire. "One thing my little girl will need to have is stoic endurance of both pleasure and pain."

Her eyes fluttered as she grappled with the mounting hedonism at the apex of her thighs. "Please, not again."

"Yes, again," I insisted, sliding two fingers into her glorious sex. I inhaled sharply at the feel of her incredible warmth, already imagining how amazing my cock would feel in place of my fingers. As if it heard my call, it swelled. "This time, I want to enjoy you."

"Oh!" Twisting in my binds, her body arched, but rather than fighting to be free, she planted her heels into the mattress and splayed her knees as wide as the bar at her ankles would permit. "Oh God, yes." Head lolling back, her eyes fell closed as her lips parted.

"You like that?" Who was I kidding? Of course, she bloody liked it! The woman was giving me every sign in the book, and her sex clenching around my digits was the final clue I'd been looking for.

"Please, more." She barely managed the words, her brow furrowing as I sped up the pace of my digits. "Faster, Master."

"Fuck." Leaning over her enticing form, I fucked her cunt, pumping my fingers in and out as the vibrator pushed her right over the precipice for her fifth orgasm. "Very nice."

She jerked as I withdrew from her sex, her whimpers frantic as I brought them to my face.

"You smell incredible."

Her gaze flitted open at the praise, her blush growing as she acknowledged my sliding the same fingers that had just fucked her between my lips.

"You taste even better." I sucked her juices from my skin, my cock straining to invade her wet spaces.

"I can't take anymore." She blew out a breath, finally meeting my gaze. "Please, Master. I'll do anything you say, but please, no more."

"You beg beautifully," I enthused, tracing the outline of her budding nipple. "It will be one less thing for you to practice." I smiled at her, genuinely thrilled with her progress. This was all new to Tiffany, and I understood it would take time for her to learn to please. Any success at this early stage was to be praised.

Her eyes filled with water, the tears spilling. She gasped, and a throaty whimper escaped as her hips rocked in time for the next burgeoning climax.

"Hush." I caught the water with my thumb, wiping the emotion from her cheek as she screamed in ecstatic torment. Watching her, I knew one thing for certain, no one had ever looked better. "No more noise, or I'll be forced to gag you."

My gaze flitted to the ball gag, patiently waiting for its chance to be useful.

Lips parted, her tears streamed, though she made no further sound.

"Good girl," I crooned, reveling in the scene as orgasm number six tore through her spent body. "I'll make sure that by the time you're allowed to sleep, you'll have never known a sense of peace like it."

Reaching for my phone, I flicked back to the camera and hit record. Her silent desperation was even hotter than all the sounds and fuss she'd made before, and I stroked my excitement as she pulled against the straps at her wrists. With this scene, I was replicating one of her favorite and most-watched internet plots. Watching her agonized expression, I wondered if it was playing out the way she'd imagined all those times she'd brought herself to orgasm. My only hope was the reality had done the fantasy justice.

I settled into her easy chair, relishing the look of her seventh and eighth orgasms. My balls ached as the scent of her arousal taunted me. I had to have her, had to know how good she felt as I buried my shaft inside her hot, wet channel. I wasn't sure how much longer I could wait.

"Beautiful." Flicking off my phone's camera, I wandered back to the bed and tugged her right nipple until fresh involuntary moans escaped her throat.

"Please." Her voice was a strained whisper, and my cock pulsed at the tantalizing raspy whimper.

"What did I tell you?" I grabbed the dormant ball gag and thrust it between her vulnerable lips. Mouth parting for her ninth trip to the stars, she had little choice but to allow the ball in place, but her eyes widened in protest.

"Ooh!" She moaned around the ball as I forced the strap around her hair and tugged the buckle tight. "Eeese."

"I told you to be quiet." My tone was stern, despite my heady excitement. "Because you couldn't do as you were asked, you'll be gagged while you reach double digits."

# CHAPTER 16: TIFFANY

Somewhere after eleven climaxes, I lost count, my brain shutting down as if it needed to preserve what little sanity I had left. Kade gagged me, as he'd promised. My jaw ached, along with my limbs and swollen clit, but ultimately, each flicker of pain merged into one tumultuous ordeal.

I'd never known pleasure could be used as a fiendish weapon, never appreciated the intensity of the torment. Sure, I'd watched the scenario for my own gratification on numerous occasions and was overwhelmed by what seemed like the naughtiness of the penance, but none of those self-induced orgasms prepared me for this.

Amid the frenzy, I slipped into unconsciousness. My sleep was punctuated by dark and disturbing dreams, vivid enough to convince me that when I opened my eyes, this whole thing would have only been a nightmare, but when my lids finally flickered to life, there was no such reassurance.

My bedroom was warm, the pale light of morning streaming in through the blue curtains I'd painstakingly chosen. Aware the gag was no longer forcing my lips wide, I smiled, certain Kade and the whole trial had been nothing but a twisted figment of my sordid imagination. However, when I rolled to one side, the solace came crashing down on top of me. There was something tight around my neck, not restrictive enough to cause breathing problems, but snug enough I was conscious of it. I lifted my hands, fumbling with the collar.

"Good, you're awake."

My heart almost stopped at the sound of his voice. I knew in an instant, without needing to turn around, that it was him—Kade was there. It hadn't been a dream.

"I kept the bondage to a minimum while you slept."

I scrambled to face him, drawing my legs up to my body in a pathetic attempt at defense, but I already acknowledged it was futile. This man had overcome me and demeaned me. There was no telling what else he might do.

"I figured you needed the rest." His shadow loomed over me, reminding me just how large the man was. "You should thank me."

"Th-Thank you." Then, as if he'd tutored me for years, the word he wanted was on the tip of my tongue. "Master."

"Very good."

I wanted to recoil at his appreciative tone. I should have done. Why didn't I?

"You remember my expectations."

My heart hammered as he reached for me, one long arm finding me in the gloom and grazing a feathery touch over my collarbone.

"You were magnificent last night." The resonance of his low tone washed over me. "I lost count of how many climaxes you had. Your body was still jerking even after you seemed to have fallen asleep."

My face blanched. Was it even possible to come when you were unconscious?

"At some point, I took pity on you." He chuckled as if there was anything amusing about my plight. My toes curled in the covers at the idea that perhaps he thought there was. "I have an hour or more of video evidence of how you looked as you were forced to cede to the vibrator." His laugh deepened. "It's very pretty."

"Oh my God." Heat bloomed in my cheeks. "What are you going to do with it?"

"What was that?" His hand rose to my throat in a heartbeat, his fingers skimming the collar around my throat.

"M-Master." I forced out the word, my head struggling to keep up with my plight.

First was the realization this was actually happening, then the acknowledgment I was not only still bound but at the mercy of a man who insisted I call him master. Now came the insidious certainty he had the most agonizingly embarrassing footage of me. Somewhere in the back of my mind, I recalled him recording me with his phone as I writhed and begged. Oh God. I never wanted to see that video, but the idea of him showing anyone else was soul-destroying.

"If you're good, I won't do anything with it." His fingertips brushed under my chin, forcing my attention back to his face, then he leaned closer.

"What do you mean by good, Master?" Did he expect me to use the word after every sentence?

"I mean obedient."

My eyes fluttered closed, the heat of his breath as oddly alluring as it was unexpected. This couldn't be possible. It wasn't happening. I had to be rational. There was no way I was even vaguely enticed by a man who lied, deceived, and manipulated the way Kade did. It didn't matter that his touch was gentle. I knew how destructive it could be. I couldn't allow his murmurs to fool me. The man had still broken into my home and taken me prisoner.

"Do as you're told, and everything will be okay."

"Please." I pulled in a shaky breath, conscious of the leather at my neck and his sudden proximity. "What do you want from me?"

"Don't you remember?" His laughter danced around me as. "Let me sit down, and we'll talk." His free hand landed on my knee and slid between my knees, edging them apart.

I whimpered as he directed my right leg to splay, conscious I should resist yet terrified of what would tran- spire if I tried. Yes, I decided—that was it—fear compelled me to conform. It definitely had nothing to do with the way my pulse quickened at his touch or the butterflies zooming in my tummy. I was *not* aroused by his show of predatory dominance.

"There we go." Pride bloomed in his voice. "I knew you could be good." Settling my left leg over his lap, he inched up the bed toward me. "You are beautiful."

Oh God, I could sense the heat burning in my cheeks. What was I supposed to say?

"Thank you, Master." In the end, I conformed, giving him what he wanted and loathing myself for the concession.

"You have amazing legs." The hand that had held my chin fell, skimming over my left breast en route to my thigh. "They'll look even better wrapped around me."

Had he really just said that? The sound of my gasp filled the strained silence, broken only by his gleeful laughter.

"As to your question, we talked about this last night."

"I…" My voice trailed away as I struggled to recall. "I don't remember."

"You don't?" Kade's head tilted in the half-light, his

features still hidden in the shadows. "Maybe it was all that pleasure?"

His fingers trailed an invisible line up my inner thigh, my breath catching as they neared my sex. I sensed how wet I was from the repeated climaxes. Christ, what if he'd checked and discovered it for himself? Fleetingly I wondered if he'd done anything else to me while I'd slept, my belly churning at the thought. It would have been easy enough for a man in his position—a man with all the power. I clenched the muscles at the apex of my sex. There was no evidence that he'd over-stepped that line, even though his every fiber seemed focused on doing so.

"I'm sorry," I flustered. "Maybe."

"You are adorable." His fingertips paused an inch from my labia. "You're so perfect for me. That's why I chose you, Tiffany."

Oh God. He'd *chosen* me?

"I know the things that get you off and know you'll enjoy what I have in store for you."

"But I can't stay like this." Panic pinballed in my mind. "I have to work, have to get ready for—"

His hand rose in a flash, one finger pressing against my lips and silencing me.

"You need to stop overthinking." His tone was calm, though I sensed an undercurrent of irritation, as though I'd spoken out of line for voicing an opinion. That idea resonated deep in my core. That was the perilous position I found myself in. No doubt Kade didn't even want me to *have* a view, let alone voice one. "Remember what I asked of you."

I panted around his finger.

"What was it, little girl?"

"To obey."

His finger moved away as a reward for the right answer.

"We will take care of those things." His voice had a peculiar calming quality. "I don't want you to worry about them."

"Okay."

What was I saying? It wasn't okay. I had responsibilities, for God's sake—a career I'd worked hard for and cases to work on. I couldn't stay here, playing his perverse games. It didn't matter how good they sounded in my head—last night had shown me the reality. I'd never survive life with a man like Kade. I had to find a way to escape his clutches, had to get out—

"Okay, *what*, little girl?" This time his voice was almost playful.

"Master." I swallowed, my eyes closing as if saying the word was giving consent, as though I was offering him permission to tie and humiliate me. That simply wasn't true. I didn't even know Kade, and the fact we might share similar sexual fantasies was irrelevant. He was dangerous—every fiber of my being told me so.

"We'll be okay." He leaned closer, resting his temple against my crown. "Do as you're told, and I will make all of your dirty fantasies come true, but you must address me properly."

Oh my God.

"Yes, Master."

"You'll be permanently wet for me." He shifted, breathing in my scent as his hand rose to tilt my chin left and then right. His thumb stroked my cheek, apparently seeking to reassure, although his words tore through any facade." My own personal little frantic whore."

The caress of his skin was warm and undeniably tantalizing, and as the light in the room grew, magic swirled in his eyes, but beneath the alluring glint, I wondered. What sort of man would concoct a scheme like this? What man could think this was acceptable?

"You'll be good," he brushed lips over my mouth. "Won't you, little girl?"

My head spun as his hand fell to the collar on my neck, forcing me to stay as he planted a chaste kiss on my lips.

"I'll try." I didn't know what else to say.

"Yes, you will." Glee oozed from his voice. "You'll do more than try, Tiffany, or you'll find your antics posted all over your social media. I'm sure your peers and colleagues would just love to see what gets your hot pussy wet and excited."

# CHAPTER 17: KADE

I wanted to capture her expression in my mind, to burn it into my psyche for all time, so I could retrieve it whenever I chose to glory in its perfection. She was lovely, beautiful, and intelligent—the most tempting woman of all. I meant what I'd told her—her natural proclivities were so aligned with mine, it almost made me believe in a Maker. My lips curled at the preposterous thought. I knew it was nonsense. There was no greater power in the universe than what I yielded over Tiffany.

"Open your legs wider."

I inched back, my gaze falling to her delectable pussy. I'd spent hours last night watching it convulse and cream, hours imagining burying myself inside, yet I'd held back, resisting the urge to take what was mine. I realized I wasn't much of a romantic but wanted our first fuck to be more than that, to be worth something.

When she didn't comply, our eyes met, and her large, terrified gaze drilled into mine.

"Please don't hurt me, Master."

I pulled in a deep breath, fighting for composure. "You have a much greater chance of hurt *if* you resist me."

She bit her lip, struggling with the conundrum, though I didn't know why. There was no mystery. My request was simple enough. I watched as she forced her thighs to separate.

"Better," I praised. "Now, lean back on your pillow."

If it was possible, her eyes widened, but slowly, she obeyed. Running my fingertips from the back of her knee to her sex, I trailed a caress over her waxed lips. My cock sprang to life, responding to my proximity but also to her soft, damp skin.

"You're still wet." I grinned, reveling in her complete perfection.

"Oh." Her reply was a breathy pant.

"Don't say it like that," I chastised. "Like it's a bad thing. It's hardly surprising after so many orgasms." My gaze flitted to her reddening face. "I'll need to make sure I keep you hydrated. You must be thirsty."

She nodded fearfully, her doleful expression tugging at whatever remained of my heartstrings.

"Answer me." Of course, there was no need to make her say the words out loud, but if there was a God, he knew what a sick fucker I was. I couldn't help myself.

"Yes, Master."

"Do you still keep bottles of water in your bedroom mini-fridge?" I gestured toward the unit, knowing full well she did.

"Yes," she sniffed.

"Promise you'll stay put if I get you one?" My eyebrow arched with my wry tone. I had the woman tied to the bed by her neck. By the time she figured out how to deal with that, I'd be right back by her side. Tiffany was going nowhere.

"I promise."

My balls contracted at her whimpered vow. Nodding, I rose, leaving her tempting sex and going to the tiny refrigerator. I glanced back before I lowered to my haunches and opened the door, retrieving one of the three bottles inside.

"Here." I unscrewed the bottle top as I wandered back, pleased to see she hadn't moved a muscle. Handing it to her, I signaled for her to take a sip. "Drink," I instructed. "I want you well."

Her brow rose as if she begged to differ, but wisely, she secured her alluring lips around the end of the bottle and did as she was told.

"Thank you," she whispered, then drained the bottle.

"Just imagine." I settled between her legs, grazing my finger over her smooth pussy as she enjoyed the water. Her breaths came harder and faster as I circled her clit. "Imagine all the wonderful things we're going to do together."

Her hips jerked as I skimmed her sensitive nub. It had worked hard last night and was no doubt still sore and sensitized.

"I can't, Master."

"We've been through this." I sighed, vexed that her rambling was ruining the mood. I would have to keep her gagged on a more permanent basis if she couldn't learn to be quiet. "You can and will do as you're told."

Our eyes met as she lowered the bottle to her side. For one scintillating moment, I thought she was going to do something stupid, like smashing the damn thing over my head. I saw the fantasy playing out in her blue gaze, saw it repeating over and over like a scene from a movie, but her intent dwindled. I noticed the moment it was extinguished as though my stare alone had dowsed the flames of rebellion.

"Give me the bottle, little girl."

She handed it to me without complaint, and maintaining eye contact, I took a swig.

"You need a shower." I smiled, excited beyond belief at the chance to be naked with her. "We both do."

"I…" Her voice trailed away as if she'd decided whatever answer she was going to give would not be acceptable.

*Clever girl.*

"I'll untie you from the bed, but you'll wear your collar in and out of the shower."

Her brow furrowed. "O-kay."

"The correct answer is *yes, Master*," I warned, placing the near-empty bottle on the floor. "The next time I have to correct you, you'll be punished."

"Yes, Master." She blew out a small breath, her gaze falling to her lap.

"Good. I have the perfect leash for you."

My lips twitched as my gaze traveled to the bag I'd brought down to her bedroom while she slept. One day, she would understand just how much work had gone into making her fantasies a heady reality.

"Leash?"

Christ, she barely got the word out. This was going to be so much fun.

"Yes, little girl." I rose over her, tugging sharply on her hips and sending her flat against the mattress. "The chain securing you to the bed has done a good job, but you need to be leashed, just like the women in all those scenes you enjoy."

Fresh heat pooled in her cheeks as I straddled her, catching her frantic wrists and pinning them above her head. They went with little fight, whatever resistance she offered crumbling under the weight of my might. Tiffany spent too much time working and not enough time looking after herself. She wasn't as fit or strong as she might be, but even if she'd been pushing one hundred and eighty pounds, she wouldn't have been able to outmaneuver me. I was bigger, stronger, and had crafted this scheme to perfection. I would easily win.

"Thank me," I growled, regretting my desire to remain clothed while she slept. If I'd been naked, my cock would have happily slipped into her wet cunt right about now—a fact she seemed perilously aware of as her legs sought to close.

"Thank you, Master," she squeaked.

"Once we're showered, I'll put the spreader bar back in place," I smirked down at her. "Then you'll have no choice but to be open and available."

"Oh God."

"You keep saying that." I frowned. "I wasn't aware you had any religious beliefs." I'd watched her for so long, surely I would have picked up on prayers or bible readings by now?

"I'm just afraid, Master," she admitted, though I sensed how much it riled her to do so.

"You have no reason for fear." Though that was a rather subjective assertion. "Obey me, and I will worship you." Lowering over her, I nudged her knees wider with my legs. "Keep your hands where I put them," I warned. "If I see them move, I'll take my belt to your ass before we shower."

"Your belt?" Her breathing was ragged.

"That's right."

"Yes, Master."

Smiling, I released my grip on her delicate wrists and focused my attention on her delicious breasts.

"These are amazing." Gathering her mounds with both hands, I squeezed them together, massaging them roughly before lengthening her beading nipples. "They're going to be great to fuck." Just like the rest of her. "Soon, you'll know what it's like to be nothing more than a vessel for my pleasure." I caught her eyes, relishing the moment my words hit home. "I know it's what you've always wanted." Pinching her buds, my cock strained as she cried out. "What you need."

"Yes, Master."

I ignored her croaky tone, wrapping my lips around her right nipple and drawing it into my mouth. Christ, she was incredible, her skin so soft and her tits so firm. I wanted to devour them before clamping them and forcing my cock between them. Tweaking her lonely nipple, I drew the other into my mouth, sucking hard until her body arched from the bed.

"Yes," I murmured, shifting my concentration to her other nipple. Repeating the process, I stimulated them both, disregarding my cock's calls for satisfaction. Once we were in the shower, I would have her on her knees, taking care of my needs, but for now, I wanted to revel in this moment of sensual triumph. She was mine—these tits belonged to me— and it was about time she acknowledged the fact.

"Whose tits are these?" Forcing myself from her tempting chest, I rose over her like a god.

"Yours, Master." No hesitation this time, and so far, it didn't look as if she'd moved her arms. Good—signs of real progress. Tiffany was doing better than I'd hoped.

"That's right." I rubbed my excitement through my pants, taking in the glorious sight of her. Stretched out, naked, and at my mercy, Tiffany was all my Christmases come at once. I could scarcely believe everything I'd worked for was finally coming to fruition. "Don't you forget it."

A part of me wanted to kiss her, claim her mouth if I couldn't fuck her, but I insisted on abstinence. My glory would be all the sweeter for having waited. Leaping from the bed, I went to my bag and found the longer leash while I nursed my hard-on. Turning back to her, I ran the chain through my fingers as I approached, waiting for her gaze to settle on her latest fate.

Grabbing her hair, I moved it away from her neck and quickly unattached the D-ring that secured her to the bed. The chain would no doubt prove helpful later. Attaching the new leash, I tightened it until she was forced from the bed.

"Better." Closing the distance between us, I swatted her ass playfully. "This is where it begins." I looked her in the eyes as I made the promise. "This is where you have to work for your pleasure. No more excuses, no more lies. You're mine, little girl… all mine."

She heaved in a shaky breath, and as she released the air, I noticed a solitary tear fall from her eyes.

"On your hands and knees," I ordered, watching as she lowered to the carpet. I'd expected some conflict, but it seemed little Tiffany was totally overwrought. Good. By the time she came to her senses, I'd have her conditioned to within an inch of her life. She would be my cumslut, whatever her thoughts on the matter.

"You're going to learn what it's like to clean your master." I laughed, tugging her toward the enormous en suite. "Let's get you into the shower, little girl."

# CHAPTER 18: TIFFANY

Like my hottest dream and worst nightmare rolled into one six-foot strapping frame, Kade stalked toward my shower, dragging me after him. I scrambled behind, struggling with any composure on my hands and knees. As it transpired, all those women on the internet had made crawling look substantially easier than it was. My ungainly movement probably looked as awkward and clumsy as it felt, but there was no one there to witness my denigration. No one except him.

"Behave."

He shot a look in my direction as he attached the leather end of the leash to the hook I used to hang my silk robe from. Trapped at the end of the metal chain, I panted as he strode into the shower and started the flow of water. Glancing around, I considered my options. For the first time in hours, I was both free of his fetters and out of bed. That gave me an opportunity. I could get to my feet, grab the end of the leash and run. I knew this house after all. It was mine. Maybe I could make it to the front door, though I didn't know if Kade had taken my key. Perhaps I'd find my phone and send an emergency message to Melissa. My heart pounded faster at the thought. It had been on my nightstand when I'd gone to bed but wasn't there this morning.

*But what then?* The voice nagged as Kade shrugged out of his shirt. *He has videos of you, doesn't he? You saw him making them. What will happen when the police find them and they're used as evidence in his trial? When people discover the weird shit you're into?*

My throat dried as I contemplated that terrible outcome, my gaze rising to the end of the leash.

"I wouldn't."

I tensed at his warning, recoiling to the fancy black tiles I'd chosen as he stepped toward me. "I wasn't doing anything, Master."

"Good," he replied as he unbuckled his belt. I watched as the denim slid from his hips, pooling at his bare feet. Gaze drilling into me, he stepped from the fabric, kicking them aside. "Let's keep it that way."

The air in the bathroom seemed to evaporate.

"I'd blister your backside so hard you wouldn't sit down again this week, and I'd make sure I got the whole thing on video—for my collection."

Mortified embarrassment burned on my face.

"Tiffany." Suddenly, he was right there, towering over me. I risked a glance north, peering up past his muscular thighs to the fucking enormous erection that strained at his Calvin Klein underwear. *Fuck.* I'd forgotten how big the thing was. "Do we understand each other?"

"Yes, Master." I breathed the words in one long breath, unable to draw my attention from his cock.

"Get under the water." He nodded toward the shower, taking the end of the leash in his hand.

"L-Like this?" I stammered, unsure what he wanted. Was he really going to make me shower while leashed?

"Yes," he snarled. "Unless you want me to gag you first?"

That made me move, my hands and knees clambering to coordinate as I crawled into the huge cubicle. I recalled how happy I'd been with my choices when the en-suite had been refurbished, how long I'd spent choosing the shower and associated décor. It all meant little now I was the one on her knees under the water. He moved in behind me, closing the door and dominating the space.

"Get your hair wet." He redirected the torrent at me, and I squealed as a blast of warm water hit me in the face. "I want it washed and your legs and underarms shaved. Here." He thrust my shampoo at me, nudging the flow, so it landed on his honed abdominals instead. Momentarily transfixed, I watched as the water crashed over his obliques, cascading over his perfectly toned ass.

"Thank you, Master."

I took the bottle, excruciatingly aware that thinking about his flawless body was not helpful. This man was not my friend, nor was he an alluring lover. Kade was my captor, the man who'd hidden in my house, hellbent on taking me. I was in trouble, and it was about time I dialed down my arousal and started to act like it. Rising to my knees, I squeezed product into my palm and massaged it into my hair. It was utterly surreal showering like this. I'd fantasized about being on my knees for the right man for so long that living something close to the reality felt like a fucked-up dream.

"Do you know how long I've wanted this?" His lips curled as he helped himself to shampoo and worked it through his near-black hair.

"No, Master." My chest rose and fell as I waited for his

answer. I was painfully conscious I couldn't do anything—shave, rinse or even leave the shower—without his say so.

"So fucking long." He stepped under the water, his silver-gray eyes closing as he rinsed the suds from his hair. "I've wanted you for so fucking long."

Crap, what was I supposed to say to that? Why had he wanted me—I didn't even know the man—what was it about me he found so damn alluring? Why was I his chosen victim? His cock pulsed while the water flowed over his hard lines as though it was answering for itself.

"Do you like what you see?" He smirked, and I realized he was no longer showering. He was staring at me, watching me gaze at his erection.

"Yes, Master." Crap, had I just said that aloud? What the hell was wrong with me?

"That's good." He flashed me a smile. "Because once you're shaved, I'm going to need you to take care of this again for me." His gaze burned into my skin.

"Are you going to hurt me?" I loathed the tremble in my voice, but it was impossible to ignore.

Everything about Kade screamed he was a threat, from the way he'd accosted me to his powerful body. While a part of me was afraid to know his answer, I needed to know what his intentions were. It was one thing to talk about obedience as if I were a well-trained puppy he could lead around, but quite another to live the reality. I'd fantasized about pet play and captivity for years, but that didn't mean I wanted this—or gave him permission to treat me this way.

Daydreams were not consent, and captivity couldn't be dressed up as something sensual and exciting.

*Though it is exciting.* My eyes fluttered closed as I tried to rationalize the niggling voice in my head. *However scared you are, deep down, you still find this exciting.*

"Did I hurt you last time?"

My brows knitted as I recalled the intensity of last time. "No, Master."

"Then there's your answer." The mettle in his voice took me by surprise, his tone compelling my gaze to open. "I will never cause you real harm." His expression was serious; determined gray eyes framed by dark hair and high cheekbones. "That's not to say I won't punish you when you need it." Tugging me closer with the leash, he redirected the water flow, forcing my eyes closed as the shampoo was rinsed from my hair. "And I will condition you to my liking."

I gasped under the water, leaning forward to catch my breath.

"We both know what we like." His deep, insidious chuckle filled the air around me like the rising steam. "I know we can enjoy each other."

Just like that, the water was gone, leaving my hair sodden and falling around my face.

"Up." The word was accompanied by a sharp tug at my neck, encouraging me back to my feet. Panting and disorientated, I rose on shaky legs, flicking my hair from my face.

"Can I trust you with this?" He waved my razor in his huge palm. "Or are you going to try something stupid?"

"I won't try anything." Even standing beside him, I felt small and impossibly weak. One blade wouldn't be enough to bring down the strapping tower of muscle that was my captor. "I promise, Master."

"You promise?" His eyebrow arched as he lifted the blade toward me.

"Y-Yes."

Christ, my voice was barely even a squeak. It was insane how one man with a conniving plan could reduce me to such a sniveling pathetic excuse for a woman. Heaving in a breath,

I fought to compose myself. Hating myself would not get me out of my predicament, but it could sure make escape much harder.

"Impress me." Kade thrust the razor at me, folding his huge arms across his chest when I took it. "Use the shower gel."

He motioned behind me, and warily I glanced back to see my favorite tea-tree product in the corner. With anxiety roiling in my stomach, I reached for it, squeezing a quantity into my palm and rubbing it under my arms.

I'd shaved myself thousands of times before, a monotonous task I'd resented as much as I'd taken it for granted, but this morning everything was different. Now I was shaving under Kade's watchful eyes, each stroke of the razor judged by his ruthless stare, my apprehension growing with every cocked brow.

"And your legs." He stepped closer as I concluded my underarms, his cock jutting toward me as though removing my body hair was the biggest turn-on he'd ever witnessed.

It was ridiculously distracting to have him brooding there beside me. The man was both menacing and glorious. Nodding my compliance, I squeezed more of the gel onto my palm and started work on my right leg. By the time both were hair-free, I was almost giddy with the strained atmosphere.

"Good." His palm appeared in front of me. "Give the blade to me."

My hand shook as I laid the upturned razor in his hand.

"You did well, little girl." He smiled, although I couldn't decide if the gesture was supposed to be reassuring or not. "Now, you can answer my question."

"Master?" My whirring senses told me I'd had too many glasses of wine, but that was preposterous. I had had none.

"I asked you if you could take care of this?" Razor returned to its place, his hand slipped around his shaft, pointing his cock in my direction.

"Oh." My heart raced as I contemplated the task. I couldn't even decide if I wanted to satisfy him, didn't know if it was better to relent or resist. What was the etiquette for this crazy situation?

"And?" His voice had taken on a terse quality. "What's the answer?"

"I'll do my best, Master," I managed, but as he pushed me to my knees, a new realization dawned on me.

I'd have no choice.

# CHAPTER 19: KADE

Flicking her tongue over my crown, Tiffany's gaze flitted to mine as if she sought praise for such minimal effort.

"Keep going," I commanded, fisting her wet hair to drag her lips down my shaft. The pleasure never really began until the woman was choking around my cock, and her current pitiful attempts weren't hitting the spot.

I didn't want to sound apathetic to her endeavor. She had to absorb a lot in a short amount of time. I had enjoyed many hours of preparation, where she'd had the benefit of none. Everything I demanded was new to her, a departure from her dull little life, and while I would insist she one day thank me for the shift in gear, it was too soon for that. To bloom into the wonderful cumslut I needed, Tiffany, like the delicate orchids downstairs, needed nurture and encouragement.

Working my shaft up and down her throat, Tiffany took all of me with ease, but her desire to come up for air meant the moment of bliss where she was filled with my cock was frustratingly brief. Tightening my grip in her hair, I pushed her back to my balls, reveling in the intensity before she tried to pull away. I could keep her where I wanted her, hold her in place until I erupted down her throat, but in some ways, that defeated the objective. The whole point was taking a woman who wanted to be treated this way, not one who would fight me at every juncture. Tiffany needed training, and it was my responsibility to ensure she got what she needed.

I had just the piece of equipment that would help her, already stashed away in her attic. As the heat of her throat enveloped my hard length, my arousal soared as I imagined her tied to the contraption. I'd found the device online and ordered it while I'd taken up residence upstairs. Her long working hours had given me plenty of time to put the thing together, and now it was available to condition her hasty gag reflex.

"Yes," I gasped, holding her flush against my groin as the pressure at my balls burgeoned.

In my mind's eye, I saw her strapped to the apparatus. Fixed to the wall with a plunger-like mechanism, basically, the gadget was a black plastic dildo with fastenings to secure a willing mouth around it. Simple enough so far. The real beauty of it came not in its simplicity but in the springs attached to either side. When the wearer of the device accepted the full length of the dildo into their throat, the springs relaxed, offering no resistance, but to relieve the pressure at the throat and withdraw, the wearer had to pull against the springs, tautening them at great personal exertion.

Seeing it used multiple times on the site Tiffany liked to enjoy, I relished its unassuming efficiency. Every time the model tired, the dildo slid deeper into their throat, forcing them to take more and train their reflex to accept it. If I added simple bondage to ensure her hands were kept out of the equation, the device would do all the work for me. A few hours of training every day, alongside practice on me, would make sure she soon could take every inch of what I had to offer.

"Fuck."

That thought toppled me, the intensity of my orgasm taking me by surprise. Pumping cum into her throat, I pulled away, painting her face before gravity took the rest to the floor. I noticed a drop landing on my feet as she gasped for air.

"Not bad." I patted her head like an animal. "Don't worry, I'll help you improve."

Trepidation flickered in her gaze as she caught her breath.

"What do you say?" I prompted, unimpressed by her responses. "I just gave you the gift of my cum."

"Thank you, Master." She was hoarse as she replied, her face erupting into another beautiful blush.

"You missed some." I pointed to my right foot. "Get down there and lap it up, little girl."

Her gaze flitted to mine as if she either hadn't heard or couldn't believe the order.

"Problem?" I folded my arms across my chest.

"N-No, Master, I just..." Her explanation trailed away as she glanced down at the foot in question.

By now, there was very little evidence of my cum, but I'd already decided—she would lick my feet and show me the damn devotion I deserved.

Slowly, she fell to all fours and lowered her face to the floor. She hovered for a moment, apparently overthinking the modest task I had assigned.

"Do I need to take my belt to you?" I tapped the other foot against the shower floor.

"No." The panic in her voice was fucking glorious. "I'm moving."

Her tongue flicked over my foot a moment later, lapping at my skin. I couldn't tell if she actually managed the job, but it didn't matter. It was wonderful to see her there, face to the floor, worshipping me as she should. Mentally, I added the practice to the list of daily tasks I was concocting for her. Soon, lapping my feet, like taking eight inches in her throat, would become second nature to Tiffany.

"Excellent." I could hear the glee in my voice. "Now do the other one while you're there." I shifted my weight, offering her my left foot, and she gingerly crawled into position, humbling herself as she lapped. "And the toes," I prompted, noticing how my cock was stiffening despite its recent gratification. "Suck each one, little girl."

"Oh God." Pulling in a deep breath, she hesitated only for a second before she obeyed, parting her lips and sucking on my big toe. My cock pulsed with enthusiasm for her devotion. Watching her demean herself at my instruction was everything I had imagined.

"Mmmm, very nice," I enthused. "Look what you've done."

Her arms quivered as she rose to her knees, though her gaze stubbornly refused to look at my growing excitement.

"I. Said. Look." Grabbing her hair, I jerked her head up to meet my gaze. Teary blue eyes met mine, her face flushed with obvious disgust, though whether the emotion was directed at me or herself, I couldn't say for sure. "See how much I enjoy your attention."

Her eyes closed for the briefest moment. "Yes, Master."

"You should be proud."

Her lack of fervor riled me.

"Pleasing me is your number one role now."

"Y-Yes, Master." She seemed so small and sorry for herself. I'd expected the rush of hedonism that would come with taking and taming the beauty but hadn't counted on how much her sorrow would affect me.

"Get up." Shifting my hands to her underarms, I pulled her to her feet. Mentally strong and driven she might be, but she was a ragdoll in my hands, vulnerable to my every dark whim. "Hands behind your back."

She slid her wrists into place without complaint, her head falling as if she couldn't carry its weight anymore.

"You're going to find this much easier than you think." Reaching for her chin, I stroked her damp skin, massaging the remnants of my cum into her complexion. "Stop over-thinking."

"I don't know how, Master."

"You'll learn," I assured her. "Just as you'll learn what I expect." My hand slid to her nape, pulling her closer. Her breasts skimmed my torso, tantalizing my already interested erection. " Eyes on me."

The tension in her jaw told me how much she didn't want to conform, but eventually, her gaze rose to mine.

"Why are you resisting what you so obviously desire?"

"I don't know."

That hadn't been the answer I was expecting.

"I'm just so scared…" Her brows knitted, her gaze falling to my chest like a reflex. "I'm sorry."

My thumb stroked the side of her neck, squeezing the area possessively.

"I asked you to look at me." My voice was softer, and her attention darted to my face in an instant. "The fear is necessary," I told her. "For the time being, at least. Get used to following orders and consistently do as you're told, and perhaps there will be more consent and less coercion."

A small sob caught in her throat, her lips parting at the sound.

"I've already said I won't harm you." I couldn't understand my peculiar reaction to her plaintive responses, and frankly, it bothered me more than Tiffany's behavior. I'd known she'd be this way, must have realized she wouldn't go willingly into the darkness with me—what had I expected? There was little point in pitying the woman I'd chosen to subjugate. I had to get a grip.

"I know, Master." She blinked away tears. "Thank you."

Exasperated more with myself than her, I yanked her closer, pulling her flush against my body. She went with a yelp, but to her credit, her hands remained lodged in the small of her back.

"Listen," I growled. "I can make this good for you, little girl. I can make it better than you've ever known, better than you'd dared to dream."

"But I have to give up everything." Her voice wavered. "Everything I know."

"Yes." My voice held utter conviction. "I need all of you, not just the parts you're happy to share."

"Master." Her brow creased, and I had the sense she was at war with herself, conflicted about whether to ask her question.

"Yes." My cock buried itself at her hip, buoyed by her willingness to refer to me correctly. After so many corrections, she seemed to have accepted this one small thing. Perhaps there was hope for the depravity we both deserved.

"I'm hungry." Her gaze flitted to me, then away again. "Please, can I eat something?"

A pang of guilt echoed in my chest at her plea, a reminder taking her wasn't only about binds and orgasms. I was responsible for all of her—her health and wellbeing, as well as her sexual pleasure—and if I wanted to enjoy her going forward, I would need to prioritize taking care of her.

"Soon," I promised, turning to switch off the shower. "I've been looking forward to showing off my culinary skills."

Her brow rose. "You have?"

"Oh yes." Wrapping my arm around her middle, I breathed her in. Washed, shaved, and ready to be mine, Tiffany was my real-life fantasy. "I just have one little test for you before we eat."

Swooping, I captured her lips in a punishing kiss, coaxing her mouth to part before exploring her wet warmth. Soon it would be my cock discovering her other wet places. Soon, I would bring her to her knees for very different reasons. Tiffany had always been mine. She just hadn't known it until this moment.

# CHAPTER 20: TIFFANY

Exhaustion swept over me like a tsunami, as if every last ounce of energy had been wrung from my body. He was the one propping me up, his passion stirring what little fight remained, and though I could see his lips moving and hear words coming from them, I didn't have the strength to focus on their meaning.

"Master." In the end, the need to speak up became untenable. I had to eat something, had to revive myself before I slipped away for good in my shower.

"Yes." His cock throbbed at my hip, demanding more of the pleasure he'd just enjoyed. I inhaled, aware of its proximity and more disturbingly, unsure if I welcomed it.

"I'm hungry." I looked into his eyes, the intensity of his gaze searing me until my gaze dropped to his impressive chest. Between my breasts, the metal chain he'd attached to my neck hung loose, a mortifying reminder of my new place in the world. "Please, can I eat something?" It was humiliating to have to ask. I was in my own house, for God's sake, but there was little point pretending I didn't need his permission. Even at my fittest, I couldn't overpower a man like Kade, a wall of solid muscle and ill intent.

His expression softened, and I had the sense that wasn't what he'd expected me to say, though God only knew what a man capable of Kade's behavior was thinking. It was probably better not to know, although I'd have to learn to understand him if I was to have any hope of survival.

"Soon." He turned, switching off the shower. Thank God. The water had been running for an age. It was going to cost me a fortune. "I've been looking forward to showing off my culinary skills."

My brow rose. "You have?" He didn't strike me as the chef type, but then what the hell did I know? Kade had been hiding in my attic for only who knew how long, and I hadn't even noticed. My breathing increased as the perturbing thought smacked me in the face again—I hadn't even noticed!

"Oh, yes." His arms snaked around me, pulling me closer while his other palm tightened on the back of my neck. I was diminutive compared to him, so unprepared for whatever he had planned, I could barely catch my breath. "I just have one little test before we eat."

A test, what did that mean? I stared at him, the unvocalized question no doubt in my eyes. Kade's lips curled for a fraction of a second, his gray eyes shining as he swooped. He moved so fast, I had no time to respond. His mouth captured mine, the caress as hard and unyielding as his entire approach, compelling my lips to part before his tongue delved inside.

For a split second, I considered resisting, contemplated drawing away just enough to headbutt the asshole and bring him to his knees. If I could manage that, I could get away from the shower, and if I could achieve that, I could lock him in the cubicle, barricade the door and go for help. I saw it all in my head—my opportunity to flee and seize control of my life again, then it was gone—replaced by the tug of visceral connection the odd intimacy ignited.

I didn't want him, but I had to have him. I loathed his arrogance and physicality, yet he was everything I'd been dreaming about my whole life. The weight of the contradiction amplified in my mind until all there was in the world was Kade—his smug, overbearing need to possess me and the combined gravity of our apparent shared depravity. If he genuinely knew about all my internet searches, about the scenes and kinks that pushed me over the precipice, there was no hope for me.

It was one thing to wield his undeniable strength over me, one for me to accept I could never compete with his strapping physique, never outrun or outreach him, but another thing to recognize my own insatiable desires. He drew away an inch, leaving me gasping for breath, and as I gazed into his mesmerizing eyes, I realized something shocking.

A man like Kade could make me break all my own rules. A man like Kade could worm his way so deeply into my head, I had no choice but to succumb.

My eyes fell closed as I struggled to counter the disturbing truth. When I had been on my hands and knees, kissing his feet and sucking his toes, I'd hated it—hated *him*, his audacity and expectation shaking me to the core—but ultimately, I'd done it. I would do whatever he asked, but not because I feared reprisals, not really.

Kade frightened me, but he seemed to have a softer side, which I could possibly manipulate and win over. It wasn't the monster who would keep me in line, but the wanton part of me the monster roused. In the end, I'd debase myself because it got me hot. I'd lowered myself because I wanted the high. When push came to shove, I'd do it *to* myself.

Sweeping me from my feet, Kade opened the shower door and carried me into the bathroom. He set me on the mat and opened my bath towel, wrapping it around me.

"Dry yourself." He yanked the towel from the heated rail and stretched it around his honed obliques. His cock, ever enthusiastic, bobbed beneath the barrier.

I ran the towel over my body before lifting it to dry my hair. He eyed me intently, his analysis terrifying yet utterly enthralling. Being around Kade was like having whiplash; impossible to keep up with his changes of tack.

"I see you have a coffee maker in your room." His face twisted into a smirk.

"Yes, Master." Where was this going? After everything, did he finally want something as simple as coffee? "Can I make you one?" I cringed at my perky tone, regretting it immediately. How did I keep forgetting what was going on here?

Kade wasn't an invited guest. He was a madman who was determined on my complete debasement, and worse, I seemed inclined to put on a show for him. I had to master my own emotional responses.

"Yes." His eyes shone a brilliant silver as he gestured for me to walk back into the bedroom. "I like the idea of you serving me."

Oh, I bet he did, though as I wandered toward the foolishly expensive machine, I registered the facet of me that also liked the idea. I'd also fantasized about being useful to a man, being dehumanized until I was nothing more than a vessel for his service and pleasure. Now, right before my eyes, Kade brought that role to life, his impudence knocking me for six. I hadn't seen it coming, hadn't noticed the threat lurking inside my home. Frowning, I checked the water reservoir and reached into the small drawer of coffee pods.

"Which coffee would you like, Master?" Christ, it was scary how easy that word rolled off my tongue. Licking my dry lips, I ignored the realization, trying to focus on the man I needed to keep on-side if I wanted to get through this.

"Something powerful." He eyed me, his lips still curled into a smirk. "I like it black and strong."

Resisting the urge to make a quip that might land me in even more trouble, I concentrated on the selection, choosing an intense Americano, and started the machine.

"It should only take a minute," I announced, twisting to meet his knowing gaze.

"Good," he answered. "Lean over the dresser while you're there. Make yourself appealing."

Brow furrowing, I scrambled to please, the thought both satisfying and riling.

"Legs apart." He swatted my ass, and I leapt at his sudden proximity, not noticing his approach. "Hands on the counter. Arch your back."

"Yes, Master." I planted my palms on the dresser and stuck my ass in his direction, despite the call of my rational mind not to indulge him.

"Lovely."

His tone was appreciative and more rewarding than it had the right to be. I panted as his hand traveled across my tensed orb, dipping between my cheeks and skimming a line over my pussy. I was wet, just as I'd been since he'd pulverized me with the cruel vibrator. Kade was as ruthless as the plastic had been, relentless and completely unwilling to back down.

"Your coffee, Master." I gestured to the cup about to overflow.

"Allow me." He chuckled, switching off the flow before his hands returned to my body. One trailed a line along my inner thigh while the other snaked around my breasts, squeezing my right mound firmly. I slumped against him, humiliated to know, despite his every menacing suggestion, he could still affect me so much. "There." He breathed the word into the side of my neck. "That's better, isn't it?"

"Yes, Master." I didn't even know what I was agreeing with. I only knew I wanted more of this growing sensuality and less of the tyrannical madman who was resolute on my destruction—disregarding the fleeting thought they could be the same thing.

"Good girl." His fingers shifted, skimming along my skin until they were in position. The palm at my breast rose, elongating my desperate nipple, while the hand at my thigh slipped to the apex, sliding between my swollen labia. "You're almost as frantic as you were last night."

My head fell forward as shame rolled over me in waves.

"Head up." His voice was terse. "You don't move unless I say so."

Righting myself as two of his digits slipped into my sex, I gasped as he finally filled me. I shouldn't want this, should fight him and not brazenly offer myself, but oh God, he was so good, the way his fingers stroked inside me before pumping in and out—it was everything I'd missed, everything I needed.

"Stand up straight."

Panting, I struggled to obey as his fingers played me like an instrument.

"Good girl."

I stiffened at the sound of his amusement, inadvertently clenching around his fingers.

"Oh, yes," he praised, nuzzling my neck. "I like that. Do it again."

Pulling in air, I obeyed as the pace of his fingers intensified.

"I love your tits," he enthused, sliding his hand to my left nipple and pinching.

"Oh God." Much more of this, and I would lose myself to the pleasure.

"Master will do, little girl."

I tensed at his laughter, but rather than putting me off my stride, it only fueled my desire. I liked it when he humiliated me, and being used on a whim was hot as hell.

"Do you want to come, little girl?" he purred into my ear.

"Yes, please, Master." I didn't hesitate to reply, the pursuit of passion my only thought as his palm skimmed my eager clit.

"How badly?"

Why was he playing with me? Last night, he wouldn't stop the damn pulsing plastic from making me come, and now, he was taunting me with the prospect. The man was definitely a sadist.

"Very badly."

"Tell me." His soft growl lingered in my ear. "Beg me for your release."

"Please," I gasped, unsure what else to say as his fingers intensified the pressure at my core. "Please let me come."

"Master," he corrected.

I could tell he was enjoying himself. Although I couldn't see his expression, I imagined his face lit in an arrogant leer.

"Please let me come, Master." I was so close now. Another

few seconds of stimulation would do it, sending me soaring to the stars. I'd sworn last night I never wanted pleasure again, never wanted to feel another impending orgasm, but I'd been wrong. It was within my grasp, and I sought it with open arms. "Please."

My knees buckled as the hedonism impended, my legs unable to tolerate the passion. Kade held me in place, his frame controlling my stance, just as his fingers mastered my pleasure. Pushing my hips toward his palm, I sucked in air, knowing the climax wouldn't save me or set me free, yet craving it all the same. It was mine. I'd earned it. I—

My thoughts splintered as his digits slipped away, bringing my imminent pleasure to an abrupt halt.

"No," I panted, my eyes wide as the hand that had been rocketing me toward ecstasy grazed my hip and steadied me. "No, please!" My clit throbbed voraciously, frantic for the final few caresses it needed to fly.

"Yes, little girl." His dark laughter taunted me with its sickening malice.

How could he do this? Why take me so close, then leave me dangling? It was worse than insisting I come, meaner and more debilitating.

"That's just a little lesson about denial. I own your orgasms now, which means I decide when you come and when you don't."

Collapsed against him, enraged yet too weary to move, I couldn't believe he'd done it, couldn't see the sense in denying me, then it struck me. The denial was like every-thing else—about power and control. Kade had control, and what did I have? The question pinballed around my head, though the answer was obvious. *I had nothing.* The void that had opened in the pit of my stomach stretched until the black abyss was encompassing. I had nothing. This man had crashed into my life and left me with nothing.

"Fuck." I had no idea if I actually said the word aloud, the only clue being the increase in his sinister laughter.

"On your knees," he instructed, guiding me to the floor. "It's time for your test."

# CHAPTER 21: KADE

Tiffany was every inch as wonderful as I had dreamed. The desperation flickering in her eyes was the ultimate aphrodisiac. Sipping my coffee, I grabbed the end of her leash and settled myself in her nearby easy chair. The chain between us tightened as I beckoned her forward. Lifting her head, her huge watery blue eyes met the gesture.

"Don't look at me like that." It wasn't anger that swirled in my tone but amusement. If Tiffany thought she could sway me with her puppy dog eyes, she could think again. "Denial is good for you, and we both know you love being treated this way."

Her brows knitted, though sensibly, she didn't respond.

"Now, move." Even now, my voice was soft. "Before I add punishment to your daily list of tasks."

She scuttled toward me, her dark waves falling over her face. Lifting the coffee to my nose, I breathed in the satis-fying aroma. This was how every morning should begin—a shower and an orgasm from my beautiful new cumslut, then coffee with my personal footrest. My lips twitched at the enticing plan.

"Stop feeling sorry for yourself." I reached for her cheek, running my fingers along her heated skin. "You'll get used to the way I do things."

Hurt glimmered in her eyes, but as I looked into them, there was something else, as well—a glint of the woman who had longed for the treatment.

"Remember where I put your toys?" My eyebrow arched as I questioned her.

"Yes, Master." Her gaze flitted in the right direction.

"Go there and find me your gag, lube, and butt plug."

"But M-Master." Her brow rose. "I didn't complain, and I—"

"Stop." The fingers at her cheek slid to her lips, silencing her. "Stop before you get yourself into trouble." Tiffany's eyes were huge as my hand shifted to the chain between us, tugging her closer. "This is not a punishment. It's what I want while I drink my coffee." I locked gazes with her, and she pulled in a breath.

"I just—"

"You're just overthinking," I snapped, irritated to have to explain this to her again. "You only have one thing to remember, one rule to follow. What is it, little girl?"

"To do as you tell me." Oddly, she seemed to relax with the admission, her shoulders falling as though some of the weight had been lifted with it.

"There you go." I offered her a smile. "I knew you hadn't forgotten. So, what do you need to do?"

"Fetch the things you asked for, Master." Her gaze fell, flitting to the place beside her bed where I'd left the items.

"Go then." I dropped the end of her leash. "Don't make me regret the decision to let you move around."

She nodded, catching her lower lip between her white teeth.

I watched her crawl away, her hips sashaying as she rounded the end of the bed. Briefly, I contemplated whether the plan was reckless. Technically, she could be on her feet and away in a matter of moments. She could be out the door and disappear into the house.

Calm down. I inhaled my coffee, reassuring myself. I had all the bases covered—the key to the front door and hours of humiliating video evidence to use against her. Tiffany would not be going anywhere. As if she sensed where my thoughts had gone, her hands and knees paused as she glanced over her shoulder.

"What are you doing, little girl?" I sipped my drink, searing her with my gaze.

"Nothing, Master." Her face blanched as she turned back and slunk around the side of the bed.

My passion grew as I waited. I couldn't see what she was doing from here, but I envisaged her collecting the toys, imagining her trepidation as she worried about what I would do with them. Tilting my head, I noticed her inching open the bottom drawer of her bedside table.

"Have you found them?" I prompted, certain I had left the necessary items on the carpet waiting for use. My brow furrowed as I struggled to recall. It had been one hell of a night, and in the end, I'd only had a few hours of sleep. Maybe I'd put them away. Anxious to plow on with her debasement, I shifted in my seat. I couldn't wait to use her as my footrest, and once she was suitably plugged at both ends, I would take my time and revel in her denigration.

"I see them, Master." Her tone had an edgy quality, an almost imperceptible difference that stirred my unease.

"Bring them here," I ordered. "Punishment can still be arranged if you can't behave."

She slowly turned, shuffling along the edge of the bed. It should have been scintillating to sit and watch her crawl for me, the leash I controlled her with hanging between her delectable breasts, but something about the scene didn't seem right. The deference had gone from her stance, the fear that once fluttered in her eyes replaced by something else —what?

Shifting toward her, I waited for her to approach, waiting to enjoy the final few moments of her subjugation before I grasped her leash and prepared her as a footrest. She lifted her head, her gaze loaded with that new emotion, and suddenly, it came to me—*defiance*.

Her narrowing eyes communicated it in a split second— the briefest warning of what was to come. By the time I'd registered the look, she'd leapt to her feet. Heart racing, I searched her angry expression for an explanation. Even though I'd just predicted the potential scenario, I couldn't believe she was stupid enough to defy me. I refused to accept the betrayal.

Fumbling with my coffee, I placed the cup on the ground, ready to jump to my feet and overpower her, but before I could achieve the feat, Tiffany was on me, and something sharp was pressed to my neck.

"Don't move a fucking inch."

I didn't even recognize her voice.

"What are you doing, little girl?" There was still conviction in my voice, despite her apparent ascension.

"Taking. Back. Control." She jabbed harder, and edging in her direction, I made out the blade of what looked like a kitchen knife.

"Now, where did you get that from?" Spirals of panic

surged in my mind, but they were subdued by a peculiar sense of intrigue. I'd had no idea she was hiding a knife by her bedside, and God knew I'd spent enough time exploring the place. How had she kept it concealed?

"Turns out you don't know everything about me, *Master.*" Her brow rose, an ugly smirk painting her lips.

"So, what's your plan, darling?"

She pressed the blade harder, nicking my skin.

"Are you gonna kill me?" I couldn't bring myself to fear the woman I'd schemed about for so long. Tiffany was mine —she just needed a little help to acknowledge it.

"No." She chuckled, and if I didn't know better, I'd have sworn her voice echoed with excitement. "I just need you to bleed enough that you won't follow me."

I felt the blade as it sliced through my skin, aware of the sensation, though the pain barely registered. Tiffany lurched back as though she couldn't believe what she'd done.

Reaching forward, I captured her leash in my right hand.

"Where are you going, little girl?"

Sensing the blood coming from my neck, I lifted my free hand, and the wet warmth flooded my fingers. Shit. She'd really cut me, and like all wounds to the head, I was losing a lot of blood fast.

"Get away." She waved the blade at me again, the metal edge smothered in my lifeblood. "I mean it."

"Wrong answer." The adrenaline bursting through my veins overpowered the primal fear that should have overcome me. "This isn't how our story ends." I staggered forward, pushing her toward the door.

"You don't get to write the ending." Turning, she tried to flee, but my grip was vice-like, the chain attached to her neck forcing her to halt. Panicking, she clawed at the leather around her neck, trying to remove it as I closed the distance between us. Time moved in slow motion as I reached her, shoving her into the wall before I fell to one knee. I glanced around, briefly aware of the trail of blood all over her carpet. Like everything in this place, it looked expensive and would be damn near impossible to clean.

"Get off of me!" She sounded distraught, throwing the knife into the hall and yanking the chain at her neck, trying to dislodge the leather handle from my fingers. My lips curled at her futile endeavor. However disorientated I was, there was no way I was letting her go.

"Wrong again, beautiful." I chuckled, relishing her distraught expression. "But don't worry, I can help guide you. I'll help you, little girl."

# CHAPTER 22: TIFFANY

"Don't look at me like that."

I stared at him in disbelief. Was Kade seriously laughing at my sorrow? How fucked up was this guy?

"Denial is good for you." His lips stretched into an ugly sneer. "And we both know you love being treated this way."

My brow furrowed, a physical demonstration of how speechless his brazen cruelty had left me.

"Now, move." His voice was soft, but the taunting quality assured me he meant it. "Before I add punishment to your daily list of tasks."

I crawled toward him, hiding my face behind my dark mane of hair. I didn't want to see his smug expression or watch him enjoying his coffee while I demeaned myself at his feet. It was true the dynamic turned me on. I couldn't deny his ruthless intent had seemed sexy and blindsided me to the harsh reality of what was happening. Pressing my hands into my bedroom carpet, that actuality smacked me in the face. Kade had taken charge of my entire existence and was planning to do horrid, twisted things to me. I had to do something, had to affect inspired action before it was too late.

"Stop feeling sorry for yourself." He reached for my cheek, running his fingers along my heated skin. "You'll get used to the way I do things."

I stared into his eyes, the usual steely gray warmed by whatever entertainment he'd garnered from my torment to produce a mesmerizing silver color. There was little doubt I could dive into those eyes. In another life, at another time, Kade could be the most enticing man to walk into my life, but not like this—I couldn't accept this.

"Remember where I put your toys?"

"Yes, Master." My gaze flitted over my shoulder to my bed.

"Go there and find me your gag, lube, and butt plug." He presented the order as if it was a fait accompli, the resolve in his voice cementing something in my head. This was how Kade saw everything. He gave the instructions, and I obeyed —he'd said so himself. The nagging thought replayed in my head. I had to do *something*, stand up to his totalitarian barbarity, but what? How?

"But M-Master." My brow rose, briefly contemplating his wish list. There was no need to ask what he had in mind, but I couldn't permit this nonsense. Those things were my fantasies. They didn't belong to Kade, weren't his to corrupt and pollute. "I didn't complain, and I—"

"Stop." His hand shifted, the long fingers at my cheek sliding to my lips and pressing them. "Stop before you get yourself in trouble." His hand shifted to the chain between us, tugging me closer, and I had no choice but to scramble in his direction. Only a matter of inches separated us as he leaned toward my face. "This is not a punishment." His hypnotic gaze burned into me. "It's what I want while I drink my coffee."

I heaved in a breath, caught between the unusually strong chemistry between us and the rational part of my mind that insisted I resist.

"I just—"

"You're just overthinking." His brow creased as though he couldn't believe I'd had the audacity to respond. "You only have one thing to remember, one rule to follow. What is it, little girl?"

I knew the answer without having to think. "To do as you tell me."

My shoulders fell as if saying it aloud was cathartic. I knew precisely what he expected and understood what he was offering. So far, I'd been stunned by his approach, then bound and overawed with intensity. I couldn't let that happen again. I wasn't sure how, but I had to make Kade understand this was not okay. I hadn't asked for his attention, and I sure as hell wouldn't put up with it.

"There you go." He threw me a patronizing grin. "I knew you hadn't forgotten. So, what do you need to do?"

"Fetch the things you asked for, Master." I tensed as I parroted the right answer, ignoring the thrum of arousal the deed produced. I could no longer deny how Kade's approach affected me, but that didn't mean I had to be dominated by it. Lowering my gaze, my attention turned to the place he meant, an idea forming in my mind.

"Go then." He dropped the end of the leash, effectively liberating me for the first time in what seemed like an age. "And don't make me regret the decision to let you move around."

I nodded, my heart racing as the idea budding in my head

took shape, a tiny flicker of hope in an endless dark landscape —a chance I had to take. I'd always kept a large knife by my bedside, a legacy from the twisted horror films I'd watched as a teenager. I'd convinced myself I was safer with a weapon nearby. If I could find that, the blade could be my route out of his frenzied nightmare. Surely, Kade had to back down if I was armed? Hell, even if he didn't, I was prepared to use the damn thing. I had the rest of my life to think about. I couldn't stay a captive in my home, a victim of his every perverse whim. I had to get out of there and grab control of my independence.

Steadying myself, I crawled toward the pile of sex toys splayed across the floor. My gaze fell over the gag and plug, the items I'd once revered now redundant. The only nagging question in my plan was the location of the knife. I knew Kade had been watching me for a while—his insidious knowledge was evidence of that—but I didn't know if he'd found the weapon and confiscated it. Anxiety knotted in my belly that I might have inadvertently armed the monster. Pausing, I swallowed my trepidation, glancing back at the handsome madman who'd captured me.

"What are you doing, little girl?" Kade sipped at his coffee, his gaze piercing me.

"Nothing, Master." Come on, get yourself together. Don't lose your only opportunity to turn the tide in this twisted game he's invented.

Inching toward the toys, my hand brushed over the bottle of passionfruit-flavored lube en route to my bottom drawer. I sensed the weight of Kade's stare, though if I was lucky, his view would be obscured by the edge of the bed. *I can do this. I have to do this.* Heart pounding, I inched the drawer open, my hand disappearing until my nails grazed the edge of something metallic. *It was still there! The knife was there.*

"Have you found them?"

I leapt at his voice, but the panic only focused my intent. My fingers found the end of the blade and wrapped around the handle. By the time I heard him move, it was firmly in my grasp, dragging over the deep pile of the carpet.

"I see them, Master." Excitement bubbled in my voice, threatening to give away my secret.

"Bring them here." He sounded irate, as if making him wait was a capital offense. "Punishment can still be arranged if you can't behave."

Turning toward him, I concealed the blade along the edge of the bed as the metal chain he'd attached dangled between my breasts. His threats no longer had any impact on me. My fear and confusion had been replaced by eager nerves, frantic to wield my weapon and get myself out of this shitshow. He waited at the end of the bed, his proximity forcing my head to rise. Locking gazes with him, I realized he was no longer predatory, only an obstacle I had to overcome to guarantee my freedom.

I was on my feet in a second, switching the blade to my writing hand and closing the distance between us. Sure, I could have just tried to run for it, but I already knew that mission would fail. The best defense was offense, and Kade had inspired a particularly offensive facet of me to rise. He fumbled with his coffee cup, but I was already on him. Shoving the knife to the side of his neck, I was exhilarated.

"Don't move a fucking inch." My voice had an edgy quality I'd never known before, but I liked it and was keen to meet more of the fierce woman now in charge of proceedings.

"What are you doing, little girl?" His tone promised repercussions, but I was so buoyed by my newfound ferocity, I scarcely noticed.

"Taking. Back. Control." I jabbed the end of the blade harder as he edged in my direction.

"Now, where did you get that from?" His mysterious eyes widened, his brows knitting.

*Come on.* An urgent voice echoed inside my mind. He's stronger than you. Don't lose the element of surprise. Use this momentum!

"Turns out you don't know everything about me, Master."

"So, what's your plan, darling?"

It was so fucking satisfying to watch the stunned expression on his face, even his cocky tone couldn't ruin the moment. Pressing the end of the knife against him, I pushed deep enough to knick his skin. I wanted him to feel it, to know I was serious.

"Are you gonna kill me?" His voice dripped with disdain, enraging the warrior inside me.

"No." I forced the emotion out as laughter, wanting him to know how it felt to be mocked as you watched the situation slip out of control. "I just need you to bleed enough that you won't follow me."

With just enough force to pierce his skin, I sliced the blade across his throat. It was difficult to say exactly what I was thinking as I watched the blood spill from his neck. For sure, I wanted to be free, but I couldn't decide if I truly wanted to kill him. Panic surged at the sight of so much blood, and I staggered away from him.

Kade moved as if nothing had happened, his hand rising to the chain falling from my neck, capturing it in an instant.

"Where are you going, little girl?" His free palm shifted to his injury, his fingers covered with his life force as he drew them away for assessment.

"Get away." I waved the knife in his direction, terror ricocheting as I realized what I'd done. I'd cut him badly, and he was losing blood fast. Maybe I'd done enough damage to really hurt him, though I was still torn about how to respond to that outcome. "I mean it."

"Wrong answer." He lurched in my direction, shoving me backward. "This isn't how our story ends."

"You don't get to write the ending!" I hollered, turning to flee, but Kade's grip was unrelenting, tightening the chain attached to my neck and compelling me to stop. Clawing at the leather, I watched in horror as two of his giant strides closed the gap between us. Pushing me into the wall, danger danced in his gaze, warning me of the reprisals to follow, but then, as if the universe wanted me to have a chance, he collapsed to one knee, his focus falling to the blood-stained floor.

"Get off of me!" Desperate to be away from him, from here, I threw the bloodied knife into the hall and yanked harder at the chain. Using both hands, I frantically sought to jerk the leash from his grasp, but despite the blood pouring from his neck and his obvious growing confusion, Kade refused to let the handle go.

"Wrong again, beautiful." Somehow, despite my every advantage, he laughed at my predicament. "But don't worry, I can help guide you. I'll help you, little girl."

"I don't want your help." So enraged by his intolerable smirk, I tugged harder, finally wrenching the leash from his grip. "I don't want anything from you."

The last thing I saw before I ran from my bedroom was Kade's enormous hand reaching out for me. His palm fell to the carpet, landing on an item of discarded clothing before he crashed to the floor.

# CHAPTER 23: KADE

My last image was of her tortured expression, torn between her own desires and my bloody fate. Grabbing a black dress left strewn on the floor, I pressed the garment to my neck as I collapsed to the carpet. I knew without needing to check that Tiffany had made her choice. She'd gone, abandoning me to my plight.

The reality echoed in my chest as I struggled to control the bleeding. The first opportunity she'd had—the one moment I'd permitted her to go without restraints—she'd left me. My eyes fluttered closed at the pulverizing thought. I wasn't stupid enough to think she had feelings for me—affection, like conditioning, took time, but I didn't think she hated me this much. Hadn't I been a kind master? Hadn't I taken her deepest desires and manifested them in full technicolor? I hadn't caused her any real harm, and I'd hasten a guess Tiffany had more pleasure last night than she'd ever experienced in her life. Blowing out a breath, I clutched the cotton to my injury as I remembered her wonderful climaxes. This was how she repaid me for that hedonism—by stabbing me and running.

"You won't get far, little girl."

My voice sounded distant as if it had come from someone else, a warning I might lose consciousness if I didn't fight harder. Wearily, I reached for the towel at my waist, yanking it free and dragging it to the bleed. Pressing it into my neck, I forced myself upright against the side of the bed. I wasn't going to die here. Whatever Tiffany said, that wasn't the ending of this story.

Pushing the edge of the pain away, I fought against the encroaching numbness and compelled myself to focus on what was happening in the house. From downstairs, I heard footsteps, evidence of Tiffany's attempt to escape. The varying volume of the sound indicated she was running from one part of the house to the other, the noises sustaining me as the flow of blood pouring from my neck finally started abating.

"You can run, little girl." My lips curled, my voice stronger than before. That was promising. "Run, run as fast as you can."

"Shit!" Her panic floated through the air, meeting my grateful ears.

No doubt she'd made it to the front door and discovered it, like every other exit in the house, was locked. Every single door and window were secured, the keys tucked firmly in the bottom of my pocket. My gaze scanned the area for my clothes, finding my pants in a pile at the door to the en suite. My little cumslut had no chance of getting out of the house without coming back here and claiming those keys.

I dragged myself toward the pile, conscious she'd probably be trying the phone next. If only I was strong enough to get down there and watch her dismay as she discovered the house line had been cut, her mobile, just like her laptop, already ensconced among my belongings in the attic. The only other working device in the house was tucked safely away in the same pocket as the keys—*my* pocket. Grasping my pants, I pulled them to me, propping myself up against the bed as my hand felt the fabric for evidence of the possessions I sought. I grinned as my fingers detected them, relief spreading and lifting my senses. Everything was okay. Tiffany might have created an unexpected plot twist in my well-prepared tale, but she didn't dictate the terms. This story still belonged to me.

My head was clearer as I forced my pants on, rising to my knees as I secured the zipper. My cut would probably need stitches, but for now, I'd have to make do with the steri-strips Tiffany stored in her first aid kit. Lurching back to the en suite, I kicked the bath mat aside and headed for the cabinet. Pulling it open, I retrieved the kit and removed the bloodied towel from my wound. I couldn't help but flinch at the sight that met my eyes when I glanced at my reflection. The cut was at least three inches long, but thankfully, it wasn't too deep. It suggested Tiffany hadn't intended to kill me, only injure—a mistake she would soon live to regret. Fumbling with the strips, I did my best to secure the two sides of the lesion, covering it with a sticky dressing.

Pleased with the improvised job, I closed the first aid kit, happy once again I'd done my homework before I struck last night. I'd had all the bases covered, except for one—the knife she'd stashed away by the side of her bed. I was forced to admit, I hadn't seen that one coming, hadn't known about the weapon. I would never have imagined little Tiffany had such mettle, but I wouldn't underestimate her twice. She'd weakened me with the assault, but by the time I'd washed my hands and wandered back to the bedroom, I was resolved. Tiffany's little outburst had slowed me down, but it wouldn't stop me. She'd been a fool to think otherwise.

Walking quietly to the hall, my gaze landed on the weapon she'd dropped there, bloodying yet another of her new carpets. I shook my head as I crouched to collect it. Assessing my blood on its blade, I glanced over the galleried landing for any signs of my naughty girl.

"Oh God!" Her desperate sob was the only sign of her approach as she wandered from the direction of the back-door. "Oh God, I'm screwed."

I stifled laughter at her accurate summary of her situation. She would soon indeed be screwed, but only when I said so.

"I have to get the key."

It sounded as though she was talking to herself, psyching herself up for what she clearly knew would be a dangerous move. Evidently, Tiffany had worked out where her keys were and knew that meant coming back upstairs, where I'd be waiting, although obviously, she didn't yet know I was alive and kicking.

Quietly stepping to the end of the landing, I crouched as I watched her ascend the grandiose stairwell. It might take me a few days to persuade her, but soon, she would feel the same way about my decisions. After all, I wasn't doing anything she hadn't dreamed about. Every single act I had in mind was taken directly from her own hot little fantasies.

She turned at the top of the stairs, all her concentration on the bedroom, which she headed into without glancing back. Rising to my feet, I moved forward to the same door-way, enjoying the scene as she was forced to acknowledge my absence.

"Oh God!"

The terror in her tone was tantalizing.

"Oh God, where is he?"

"I'm right here, little girl." I wish I could have captured the look on her face as she spun around to greet me, her wide eyes and parted lips an absolute picture.

"K-Kade?"

"Forgotten how to address me so soon?" I leaned against the doorway, tucking the knife behind my back. I was feeling better by the second. "What's wrong? Did you think you'd killed me, little girl?"

"No, I…" Her voice trailed away as I revealed her weapon, her breathing ragged. "Please!" Hands raised in self-defense, she backed away from the doorway.

"I realize I might still be a little groggy, but it was pretty damn stupid leaving the knife in the hall for anyone to find." My brow rose. "I thought you were smarter than that."

Her eyes fluttered closed momentarily as if she also couldn't believe her recklessness.

"I'm sorry, Master."

Well, at least she was finally speaking to me properly, but Tiffany had to know—she would have to do a hell of a lot better if she was going to reconcile the huge fucking crater she'd created with her stunt.

"You're not even vaguely sorry, little girl." My fingers closed around the handle as I inched closer to her.

"I didn't mean it." Her gaze flitted around the room as if she expected another exit to open up from an alternative reality.

"Don't bother." I sighed. "As you've already established, there are no ways out of this house that don't involve me."

"I didn't mean to hurt you," she insisted. "I was just scared and angry."

"Well, good news." I stopped a foot away, taking in the look of her. Tiffany had clearly found a godawful coat downstairs, which covered most of her gorgeous body. "Now I'm the one who's angry."

"Please don't hurt me."

My cock roused at her plaintive plea.

"Master, I'll do anything."

"That's right," I replied. "You *will* do anything. Start by losing that coat."

Her face blanched as she shrugged it from her shoulders, and it pooled at her feet.

"You have some serious work to do to make this up to me, little girl." Reaching for the end of her leash, I yanked her closer. She stumbled into my body, her frightened gaze rising to meet mine. "Some fucking serious work."

"O-Okay."

She was so beautiful. In the short time that had passed since she'd attacked me, I'd lost sight of just how incredible she was.

"We start where we ended." I motioned to the pile of toys still strewn on the ground. "It's time you were plugged."

# CHAPTER 24: TIFFANY

This was so much worse than before. Buying myself that short period of freedom meant relinquishing it now was even harder, even more intolerable. The dark glint in his eyes told me I was in a world of trouble. He pushed me to the bed, and I went without a fuss, eying the dressing at his neck as he secured the end of the leash to my headboard.

How the hell had he cleaned himself up and got on his feet so soon? Maybe I hadn't injured him as badly as I thought. I knew blood often gushed more profusely from the head and neck. Perhaps I'd been lulled into a false sense that his wound was worse than it really was. Shit! How could I have been so stupid? I should have checked, should have slashed him harder! I panted at the grotesque thought. What the hell was happening to me? I was becoming wickeder than he was.

"Time to pay the piper, little girl." Kade spun me onto my belly, dragging my arms to the small of my back.

"What are you going to do, Master?" Panic surged through, exploding like fireworks. I'd spent so much time consumed with the ethics of my actions, I'd totally over-looked my current plight—a mistake I regretted.

"I already told you."

I tensed at the feel of ropes at my wrists, my breath ragged as they tightened. No doubt they were the same black ropes I'd purchased, the ones that had been stashed in my drawer, but they certainly seemed less innocuous wrapped around my limbs.

"You're to be plugged."

"Oh God." I buried my face in the bed as he dragged me down the covers, so my hips were at the edge, and my feet brushed the carpet. The bed dipped as he sat beside me, one hand skimming my exposed behind.

"I won't hurt you." His voice was calm and oddly reassuring. "You might resort to violence, little girl, but I won't."

My toes curled at his thinly veiled accusation. I'd said I was sorry, hadn't I? What more could I do? I knew an apology would far from suffice if I had been attacked with a knife. Guilt twisted and knotted in my tummy, persuading myself I deserved this. Maybe I needed whatever torment Kade was about to hand out.

"Hold still." Suddenly, his hand was gone, and I yelped as cold liquid landed at the cleft of my ass. He held my cheeks apart, permitting its humiliating path to my anus.

"Oh, no!" I squirmed frantically, unable to settle. He hadn't even done anything yet, but the thought of what he was going to do was utterly degrading.

"Settle down." One hard smack landed on my right cheek, and I gasped. "I want you nicely lubed." Another quantity of the cold liquid landed, beginning another humbling path between my cheeks. "Better." He sounded pleased. "Now, let's see how you take the plug. I've seen you play with it enough times."

His dark chuckle filled the air, ensuring I squeezed my eyes closed as the tip of the metallic plug nudged at my bottom. He was right, of course. I had played with the plug on numerous occasions, the taboo sessions ratcheting up my arousal tenfold, but the recognition that he had been watching all those times made me utterly wretched. Those things were private and didn't belong to him, but as he pressed the metal into my backside, it became startlingly clear there was no such thing as privacy anymore. I belonged to Kade, and after my stunt with the knife, I'd given him permission to do just about anything he wanted.

"Oh, Christ!" I panted as he inched the widest part into me, trying not to clench around it. The sensation as it wedged inside was mind-blowing, and for a moment, I couldn't decide if it was pain or pleasure I was processing.

"Good." He patted my ass as I writhed on the bed. "Now for the other end." The ball gag he'd wielded last night appeared in my line of sight. "Open."

"Master, please," I started, still struggling to accommodate the butt plug. "I—" My explanation was halted when he shoved the ball between my lips, tugged the straps around my face, and secured it unceremoniously.

"If I wasn't clear before, then let me be clear now." He leaned closer. "I don't give a shit about your opinions."

I turned at his growl, eyes wide as our gazes locked. Kade was only inches from me, his silver eyes flashing with authority.

"After everything you just put me through, this is the very least you deserve." He rose from the bed, and the next things I was aware of were the metal bracelets shutting around my ankles. It took little deduction to realize he'd secured me in the spreader bar again. He dragged me back by the hips until

I folded onto the floor, then loomed over my frantic form. "Kneel."

Slowly, I complied, trying to compose myself with the two new intrusions.

"Glorious." He towered over me, pleased. "You only need special clamps, and you'll be ready to serve."

My heart raced at his menacing assertion, my body paralyzed as I watched him choose the clamps from the floor. I'd bought them weeks ago but had been too scared to use them. He waved them in front of me as I grappled with the ropes, trying desperately to free myself.

"I love these." He smiled approvingly, shaking the clamps, so the small bells attached to them chimed. "Pretty and practical. Have you used them before? I haven't seen you with them."

*No, Master.* I shook my head, refusing to demean myself further by answering around the giant plastic ball.

"Then this will be a first." His grin grew as he lowered to my left breast, pinching the nipple until I yelped.

I wanted to plead, to beg him to stop and reconsider. The idea of him christening them for me was terrifying, but what was the point? There was no way to speak properly now, and I knew he'd never take pity on me. I'd just cut his throat. Why would he?

Kade squeezed the metal arms of the clamp open, hovering it above my beading bud. I mewled at the forthcoming agony, knowing I had no choice but to bear it. He clamped the end around my sensitive tissue, spiking a sudden hurt. Gasping around the gag, my eyes filled with tears that I resolved to ignore. I would not cry in front of him, but oh God, the clamp hurt like hell. How on earth was I going to endure it?

"Lovely." His thumb rose to my right eye, gently collecting the tear I couldn't control. "Now, the other one."

Kade repeated the process, teasing me with the threat of the second clamp before he pinched it over my nipple. I whimpered in defeat. Bound, plugged, and now clamped, I had to admit—the man had me at his mercy, and I didn't like my chances of surviving whatever came next.

"I like your chair." He nodded to the easy chair he'd been sitting in when I'd found the knife. "Hobble over there and make sure those tits chime when you move."

He was gone in a heartbeat, crouching to collect my riding crop from the floor before striding to the seat and getting comfortable. Comfort was about the furthest thing from my mind as I inched my knees forward, dragging them awkwardly against the carpet as I tussled with the relentless pain at my nipples. I couldn't believe this was happening to me, couldn't fathom how my life had boiled down to this, but as I edged toward him, Kade had become the center of my entire universe—the only one who could free me from the binds, the agony, and the urgency thrumming at my core. I hated to admit it, but he had me.

"Why can't I hear those bells?"

His eyebrow arched, the gesture tightening my furling passion. I loathed how he could do this to me but adored him for trying, for pushing me much harder than I would have pushed myself, for making me pay. This sweet agony was everything I had fantasized about, and in the heat of the moment, I could hardly comprehend everything that was taking place.

Pulling in air through my nostrils, I shook my chest, forcing the tiny silver bells to jingle at my chest. My humiliation was complete, but rather than crush me with its enormity, the concept only goaded. Kade had ignited this fire, and I wanted him to extinguish the flames.

"Better." His grin grew as I approached. "You're fucking adorable and more than qualified for your test."

He picked up the crop from my small reading table, and as my gaze followed his hand, I noticed the evil vibrator that had caused such injury last night was also waiting for me. When had he put that there? My brow furrowed. Perhaps it had been there all morning, and I just hadn't noticed. I had been rather distracted.

"Turn around." He signaled for me to move, and suspended in his web of thorny arousal, I obeyed. My head fell as he tugged at the binds at my wrists. "The ropes come off while you serve me." Kade's voice floated over my head as if he was a god. In many ways, he was more powerful than any god I recognized. "But the spreader bar and plugs stay, and if I get one whiff of rebellion, I'll keep you bound the whole fucking time we're together."

I called out when he smacked my behind, absorbing the pain and the way the impact jarred the butt plug lodged inside me. The sting transformed into something hotter and needier, my brain shifting his treatment from pain to pleasure, and I wanted more of it.

"Got it?" He leaned over my shoulder, snarling the words in my ear.

I turned my head gradually to meet the intensity of his gaze and nodded.

"Good."

My hands dropped to my sides as our gazes locked.

"I want you on all fours, your head toward the bathroom. Whenever I need to rest my feet, you have the honor of providing me with the luxury."

I moved into position, still not comprehending what he

meant but anxious not to upset him further. He lifted one, then the other foot onto the small of my back, and his meaning became clear. He wanted a footrest—he wanted *me* to be his footrest.

My head dropped as I grappled with the idea. This was one of my all-time hottest daydreams, my most searched scene on the internet—a fact Kade no doubt knew. Now it was transpiring—he was using me as nothing more than furniture.

"You're beautiful." He settled into my chair, his coziness evident from my peripheral vision. "The perfect footrest."

Steadying myself, I tried to stay calm and just breathe, ignoring my aching jaw and full backside, but I wasn't used to staying in this position. After a few minutes, I had to shift my weight from one palm to the other, my hips rocking to relieve some of the tension. The small bells chimed at the motion, highlighting my faux pas.

I never saw the crop move. The only sign the strike was on its way was the telltale swishing sound it made through the air. By the time my brain deciphered the noise, the tongue had already swatted my pussy. I yelped at the sudden hurt, panting as I struggled for composure, but even as his words rang out around me, I knew I liked the sting and was certain I craved more.

"Footrests do not move." He didn't sound angry, but neither did he sound impressed. "Every time you move, or one of those pretty bells chimes, that cunt of mine gets cropped."

Fuck, there was no way that should sound as good as it did.

"Discipline, little girl, can be painful, but it guarantees success."

Unable to swallow, I cringed as the first line of saliva

trailed from behind the plastic ball, pooling on my chin. This was the very thing that had always pushed me over the brink when I'd pleasured myself—the inability to prevent my degradation—and as it played out in real-time, my clit throbbed for Kade's attention.

"That's better." He stretched back, and I held my breath as he pulled his mobile from his pocket and pointed it in my direction. "My hot little cumslut, acting as a personal footrest for me." His voice was loaded with conceited joy as he started recording. "Let's capture this moment for posterity."

# CHAPTER 25: KADE

She'd done well, only needing another eight licks with the crop after I'd put my phone away. Relaxing in my chair, I reveled in all that I'd achieved. The plan may not have gone precisely as I'd planned, my hand rising to my sore neck as if to prove the point, but I'd adapted to the challenge and overcome Tiffany's pathetic attempt at escape. I had her now—her sweet body clamped and plugged, as it was made to be—and based on her reactions, I'd have been willing to bet she was enjoying rather than enduring the test.

The clues were there. The way her whimpers had shifted from pained pleas to throaty mewls, the slight rock of her hips when I struck her pussy as if she secretly yearned for more. Glancing down at her reddening face, my cock stirred with anticipation. Christ, she was fucking glorious, and even better, she was all mine.

"When this test is over and I've finished with you, you can message your office." I knew somewhere in that beautiful mind, Tiffany would be worried about work, conscious of the career she'd labored so hard for. "Make your excuses."

She nodded slowly, forcing out a string of blurred noises I assumed was her gratitude.

"You're welcome." Dropping the crop to my side, I reached for the vibrator, flicking on the power as I removed my feet. "You've done so well, your master wants to reward you." It made no sense to praise her after she'd attacked me, but I couldn't deny the urge to tear more pleasure from her tightly wound body, then—in my final act of destiny—I would claim her.

She moaned frantically as I slipped to my knees at her side, angling the head of the pulsing plastic at her clit and pressing it into her wet flesh. The scent of her arousal wafted to my nose as my cock strained to replace the plastic and spear her.

"Od!" she groaned, struggling to stay still. "Eeese."

"Think you deserve to come, little girl?" I tore my gaze from her delectable cunt to her face. "After hurting me?"

"Orry, Aster."

"Yes, you're sorry now, aren't you?" I chuckled at her futile reply. I tilted the plastic, nudging her clit harder, relishing the way she jerked. "Get your head down." I slapped her prone ass, leaving a pink imprint of my palm as she lowered her face to the carpet. The bells on her tits chimed wonderfully as she submitted.

"Uck, aster." She sounded frantic. "Eeese."

Climbing behind her, I kept up the pressure on her clit, releasing my zipper with the other hand. My cock sprung free, finally liberated from its fabric prison.

"Come then," I growled, increasing the intensity of the vibrator's speed. "Splinter for me, and when you do, you're mine."

Her body contracted, her gasps frantic as she grappled with the powerful wave of pleasure. I watched as round after round of hedonism crashed over her. Removing the head of the plastic, I found it soaking with her juices.

"Fuck." Cocooning her body, my cock nudged her inner thigh as I breathed into her nape. "I'm going to have you, little girl."

Lifting her head, she glanced over her shoulder as best she could, her eyes glassy with passion.

"I'm gonna fuck you because I can." I captured her damp chin, holding her there while I reinforced the point. Covered in trails of her own saliva, she looked utterly magnificent. "Because you're mine."

"Es."

Not a single word of complaint escaped her throat, her acquiescence intensifying my arousal. I'd have taken her, regardless. She *was* mine, mine to screw and enjoy, and there wasn't a damn thing she could do to stop me, but that she didn't want to was more than I could ever have hoped to dream.

Withdrawing my hips, I found her entrance as if my cock already knew the way. I slipped into her with ease, filling her with one hard thrust.

"Fuck." My balls tightened as I processed the bliss of that one incredible act. Finally, we were aligned. Finally, she had ceded, and I could enjoy her. Easing back a few inches, I slammed into her again, growling as my balls slapped against her wet pussy lips. This was the moment I'd been waiting for, that had dominated my dreams when I'd sat here alone day after day, planning her captivity.

I pounded her harder and harder until she screamed around the gag, and my senses were overwrought with desire. My body stilled as the soul-shattering orgasm erupted, splintering my every rational thought. Collapsing over her, I pushed us to the carpet, pinning her while her wonderful cunt milked the last drops of my cum.

It took a few minutes to catch my breath and process the enormity of my accomplishment. Withdrawing, I pulled her up by her hips, back to all fours. Kneeling beside her, my lips curled at the taunting tinkle of the bells.

"On your knees," I ordered, stroking my satiated cock as she obeyed. Reaching for the ropes, I bound her wrists quickly, enjoying the sounds of her disappointed whimpers. "Turn toward me."

She shuffled awkwardly, her face flushed as our eyes met.

"These can come off now." I motioned to the bells. "Much though I adore them, I don't want to damage your pretty tits." Reaching for the clamps, I released them both, watching her responses carefully. The glint of pain in her eyes was an aphrodisiac, but the grunt of hurt as blood rushed back to the sensitive tissue truly lit me up.

"You'll get used to it," I assured her, inching closer on my knees. When her gaze fell at my approach, my hand rose to her chin and forced her attention back to me. "That takes care of your test. Later, I'll punish you for this." I signaled to the dressing at my neck, exulting in her wide, terrified eyes.

"Aster." Her breaths were coming hard and fast, and taking pity on her, my finger slipped to the black leather strap. Sliding the ball from between her lips, the gag fell around her neck and rested on her collar bone.

"What?"

"I am sorry." For the first time, there was sincerity in her tone.

"You'll make it up to me," I promised her. "You'll have no choice."

Tiffany bit her lip as if she didn't know whether to laugh or cry.

"I'll punish you for your bad behavior." My hand rose to her damp, heated cheek. "But I'll also reward your good performances. You'll be safe with me, little girl. Safe and conditioned into my perfect little captive."

She nodded against my palm, her breathing still ragged.

"Can I please contact my work now, Master?"

That again. I supposed I did say she could.

"Soon," I replied. "First, I want to make a purchase."

Her brows knitted as I found my phone.

"A new orchid for your collection." My lips curled as I knelt beside her, showing her the screen.

"Y-You sent those, Master?" Her gaze rose to mine, seeking clarification.

"I did, and you didn't do a very good job looking after them, did you?"

"I…" Her voice trailed away. "They're still alive, Master."

"Because I cared for them." I laughed at her innocence. "You can't treat such a beautiful flower with disdain, little girl. It needs to be nurtured… time and attention."

"Oh." She watched as I made my selection, charging the fuchsia orchid to my account and requesting delivery for tomorrow.

"Don't worry," I chuckled, sliding my phone into my pocket. "I'll show you." She swallowed at my promise. "Soon, your fingers will be as green as your ass and tits are red."

"I don't understand." She shook her head. "Why are you buying orchids, Master?"

"I adore them." I smiled, stroking the side of her face. "You are like those precious petals, Tiffany, and I adore you for the same reason. Your beauty needs to be teased from within, and you'll only bloom in the right conditions." I laughed harder. The analogy was perfect. "Give me a few weeks to create the right conditions for you and watch the way you blossom. You won't even recognize the woman you become."

"I'm just supposed to stay and behave?" Her brow creased as if the concept was crazy. "Just do as you say?"

"That's exactly what you'll do. There's no point denying you don't appreciate my approach. Just look how wet you were when I fucked you."

Her eyes flickered closed as if she was reliving the intimacy, and I could relate. Tiffany was exquisite.

"From now on, your life is simple."

Her gaze opened, spearing me as I went on.

"You belong to me, and you'll do as you're told." I reached for her chest, tweaking her no doubt sore nipple. She gasped, shifting on her knees as she wrestled with the abrupt hurt.

"You'll do… Every. Fucking. Thing. I. Say."

The End.

**Devour Captive of Desire *for* the next sizzling installment of Tiffany and Kade!**

**Read the introduction to the book now…**

# CAPTIVE OF DESIRE

Copyright © 2022 by Felicity Brandon



## Chapter 1: Tiffany Noble

Hand trembling, I took the phone from him, accessing my contacts. Yesterday, I handled the device with swift dexterity, not even giving its use a second thought, but today, everything was different. With Kade towering over me, the power of his stare burning into my face, I could barely keep the mobile steady.

"Remember what I told you." His voice was little more

than a snarl.

"Yes, Master." Swallowing back rising nausea, I tried to focus.

"Any funny business and I'll have you bound permanently. I'm more than capable of messaging on your behalf."

The knot of anxiety twisted in my stomach. Kade was certainly capable. He'd proven that on more than one occasion, while I'd screwed up the only opportunity I'd had to be free. Struggling to catch my breath, my gaze flitted to his eyes, finding his menacing gray orbs fixed on me.

Biting my lip, my focus fell to the dressing on his neck, the evidence of my attack. *I'd done that.* The truth reverberated in my head. I'd cut him. Guilt knotted in my chest as I recalled slicing his throat with the knife. Clearly, I hadn't used enough force to do any lasting damage, but I'd wielded the blade. I'd been prepared to kill. My brow furrowed, confusion emanating at his survival. I didn't want to be a murderer, but I couldn't cope with being his captive, either. What was I going to do?

"What's the problem, little girl?" Kneeling in front of me, Kade folded his arms across his strapping chest, tightening the chain still attached to the collar at my neck. I lurched forward, steadying myself before I dropped my phone. "Why are you making me wait?"

"I'm sorry." I could scarcely think straight. "I don't know what to say."

"We already discussed what to say." His brows knitted, conveying his irritation as his hands reached for the screen. "Find your boss' contact."

"Yes, Master." Acting on autopilot, I searched my contacts for Rex's number, pulling it up on the screen.

"Now start a new message." Kade's voice had softened as he eased behind my body, straddling my legs, which were still forced apart by the spreader bar at my ankles. "I'll help you." His arms snaked around my body, grazing my aching nipples to my hands, and God help me, I arched my back into him.

*Stop that.* The snarky voice in my head screamed the warning. *Stop sending him the wrong signs.* Panting from his sudden proximity, I accepted it was too late. I'd already ceded to his desire, willingly taking his enormous cock when he'd claimed me and—to my shame—loving every moment of his possession. I loathed the things Kade stood for, despised what he'd done, but when push had come to shove, the man knew how to play my body like an instrument. He owned me in a way no one else had ever achieved before. My head spun at the disturbing realization.

Kade had screwed me, and I'd adored it. I should have been worried about our unprotected sex, should have had a head filled with fear about sexually transmitted infections and pregnancy. I should have been disgusted and outraged. *Why wasn't I?* He'd bound, plugged, and demeaned me, and instead of shriveling in fear, I'd bloomed. What the hell was wrong with me?

"How would you start a message to him?" Kade whispered the question into my nape, sending electricity sparking along my spine.

"H-Hi, Rex." I could hardly get the words out.

"Go ahead then." The hand stroking my wrist gestured for me to act, and gripping the device, I typed.

*Hi, Rex,*

"Tell him you're ill," Kade purred. "That you've been up all the night vomiting."

"O-Okay."

*Sorry I can't come to the office today. I've been ill all night, and I'm still vomiting this morning.*

"Very good."

I could hear the smile on his lips, the sound unexpectedly soothing.

"That should buy us the rest of the day at least."

"What happens after that, Master?" I turned toward him, our gazes locking.

"You let me worry about those details." His silver gaze was cold. "Remember?"

"Yes."

Kade made everything sound so simple. Rex was my boss, the man who held my career aspirations in the palm of his hand. I didn't like lying to him any more than I liked being held under duress in my house. Pulling in a shaky breath, I grappled with the trepidation churning in my belly.

"How would you sign off?"

Kade's right hand brushed past my breast. My attention lowered, watching as my flesh goosed, my nipple beading into a tight bud. It didn't seem to matter that the man had taken and tormented me, that he had no right to be here, doing the things he was doing. My body responded to him as if the title he insisted I use was correct—it recognized my master.

*I'll be in touch,*

*Tiff*

I held my breath as I finished, waiting on Kade's verdict.

"Tiff?" He snorted. "Is that what he calls you?"

"It's what most people call me, Master."

"But why?" He snuggled closer, pressing the denim of his pants against my tender ass.

Clenching around the butt plug still lodged inside me, my throat dried. I didn't like the ruthless side of Kade, but this quiet attempt at affection was just as perturbing. I never knew what was coming next.

"Tiffany is a lovely name."

"I-I don't know." I had no answers for him. I'd been known as Tiff for as long as I could recall.

"Just as well you're my little girl." His breath hot against my neck, my eyes fluttered closed as his lips brushed over my sensitive skin. "That's all I'll ever need to call you."

"Why, Master?" I croaked, conscious of how horny his show of authority was making me. My fingers tightened around my phone as if their plan was to use the device as a weapon, but I knew better. I'd wielded a much more impressive weapon and failed to achieve my aim—probably because I didn't truly know what my aim was. I wanted to be free of Kade's aggressive possession but couldn't imagine going another day without it.

It didn't make sense that his predatory tenderness should be so alluring, especially since I'd lived through his trials and understood precisely what an ordeal they were, but there was little point denying the way he affected me. Kade had discovered it for himself, especially when he'd buried his satisfying shaft inside my wet, demanding pussy. Once more, my muscles clenched at the memory.

"Why what?" he replied.

"Why am I your *little girl*?" My eyes flickered open to find him right there, his dark eyebrow arched as if he was daring me to defy him.

"Because I like it." His lips curled. "You like it too, don't you?"

*Did I?* My lips parted as though the answer would come automatically, but I didn't have a response. I'd never heard the term used sexually before Kade smashed into my life, but he had a way of making the innocuous sound sinful and dirty.

"I don't know, Master."

"Well, I do." He pinched my nipple casually, cradling my breast as his other hand slipped between my legs. Balanced on my knees with my ankles forced apart, there was little to prevent his exploration. "Drop your phone, little girl."

The device slipped from my fingers, falling to the carpet.

"Very good." His patronizing tone should have irked, but I was so caught in the rapture of his fingers as they brushed over my clit and skimmed my swollen labia, I could hardly think, let alone contemplate the offense. "Slide your hands to your thighs and keep them there."

I complied, feeling his arms tighten around me as soon as my palms rested against my legs.

"I still have to send the message, Master," I reminded him, the final fragments of my independent mind desperate to salvage whatever was left of my professional reputation. I'd never missed a day of work, had never so much as taken a sick day, and the seven missed calls from my office were a testament to that fact.

"I know." His voice vibrated as his fingertips parted my lips and pushed lightly into my pussy. "We'll send it soon."

"Oh God," I gasped, my head lolling back against him as he filled me with one, then two digits. I wanted him so much, wanted him to take control and own me as he'd done before. Kneeling there, I no longer cared if it made sense. I only knew this was the culmination of a lifetime of unfulfilled longing.

"Exactly." His tone had grown husky. "First, I remind you what happens to good little girls, then once we're both grati-fied, you'll send your message."

**Devour now!**
https://books2read.com/u/4DPxzP

# FOLLOW ME!

**Stay in touch with Felicity's new releases by** subscribing to her mailing list.
**https://felicitybrandonwrites.com/newsletter/**
**You'll also receive FREE reads just for signing up!**

**Love Dark Romance?**

**Discover ALL** The Dark Necessities **universe!**
https://books2read.com/u/mdGvJd

**Devour Tempted for FREE:**
https://books2read.com/u/b5kPPA

**Join Felicity's** Facebook group, **and Discord group, to engage with her and other awesome readers.**

www.ingramcontent.com/pod-product-compliance
Lightning Source LLC
Chambersburg PA
CBHW061252120726
48001CB00001B/270